My Phantom Husband

Also by Marie Darrieussecq:

Pig Tales

My Phantom Husband

MARIE DARRIEUSSECQ

TRANSLATED FROM THE FRENCH BY
ESTHER ALLEN

THE NEW PRESS   NEW YORK

Library of Congress Cataloging-in-Publication Data

Darrieussecq, Marie.
   [Naissance des fantômes.   English]
   My phantom husband / Marie Darrieussecq ; translated
from the French by Esther Allen.
      p.   cm.
   ISBN 1–56584–538–2
   I. Allen, Esther, 1962–   . II. Title.
PQ2664.A7214N3513   1999
843′.914 — dc21   98–55513
                                      CIP

Originally published as *Naissance des fantômes* by P.O.L. Paris
Published in the United States by The New Press, New York
Distributed by W. W. Norton & Company, Inc., New York

Established in 1990 as a major alternative to the large commer-
cial publishing houses, The New Press is a nonprofit book pub-
lisher. The Press is operated editorially in the public interest,
rather than for private gain; it is committed to publishing, in
innovative ways, works of educational, cultural, and commu-
nity value that, despite their intellectual merits, might not nor-
mally be commercially viable. The New Press's editorial offices
are located at the City University of New York.

www.thenewpress.com

Printed in the U.S.A.

9 8 7 6 5 4 3 2 1

*S*he was looking about for some way of escape, and wondering whether she could get away without being seen, when she noticed a curious appearance in the air: it puzzled her very much at first, but after watching it a minute or two she made it out to be a grin, and she said to herself, "It's the Cheshire-Cat: now I shall have somebody to talk to."

— LEWIS CARROLL

I

_M_y husband has disappeared. He came home from work, set his briefcase down against the wall, asked me if I had bought any bread. It must have been about seven-thirty.

Has my husband disappeared because that evening, after enduring years of my negligence, exasperated, worn out by his day at work, he was suddenly fed up with having to go back down our five flights of stairs, day after day, in search of bread? I tried to help the police: had it really been a day like any other? We combed through all the computer files my husband had opened since that morning. He hadn't sold anything or received anything special, he had shown three apartments, he had eaten his usual lunch, a sandwich bought at the corner store. The prospective buyers (a young couple, a middle-aged couple, and a graying divorced man, all tracked down by the police) had noticed nothing in particular beyond a faulty water heater and other fine points of real estate, that was what they were there for, they no longer even remembered my husband's face.

I was unable to provide an hour-by-hour account of his schedule, so the police advised me to dig through his mail, his desk drawers, his suit pockets, to check all the calls listed on the last phone bill he received at the office. They couldn't do it themselves: two hundred people disappear every day in this country and are tracked down, though only rarely, in the islands accompanied by beautiful blondes (as if I weren't a beautiful blonde myself), while others cross the border, in which case it's wisest to renounce all hope, and still others throw themselves into the sea, washing up bloated on the beaches, eyes and tongue eaten by shrimp, bodily crevices colonized by sea snails, it's best to spare yourself this type of reunion. The police asked me if my husband was prone to depression.

I didn't call the police right away. It was a while before I realized my husband had disappeared. I often took advantage of the time he was out buying the baguette to call my mother. I would hang up when I heard his footsteps on the fifth floor. That particular day, my mother and I stayed on the phone for a full quarter of an hour, she chattering away, me interrupting her regularly to remind her I would have to hang up soon. I had the feeling, only vaguely at first, that her story was going on longer than usual today. I looked out at the street to see if my husband was coming across; I strained to hear him in the stairway; and my mother was the one who hung up first this time, accusing me as usual of not paying the slightest attention to her, when I was simply leaning against the windowsill, wanting to give myself over entirely now to the sole pastime of calmly watching for my husband.

*T*he sun was beginning to set and I breathed in the sweet air. It was a fairly unusual thing for me to rest idly at my window at that hour of the day; generally, around seven-fifteen, I would notice that nothing was ready and race downstairs to buy something to eat (forgetting the baguette: the shop at the corner doesn't sell bread, and the nearest bakery is on the other side of the boulevard; it takes forever to cross). The rooftops were

3

turning red and the jumble of the outer
boroughs—where nothing predominates, not
slate or tile, brick or stone—blended and became almost pretty in the sunset. It was that
same evening, I didn't yet know how crucial it
would be for me, when I first noticed that
there was a flock of swifts above my impatiens, forming commas in the outsized winter
sky. Everything seemed smaller, livable, just
my size, fraudulently smaller and livable and
my size, because I could follow the flight of the
swifts as they zigzagged from one edge of the
sky to the other. The daytime haze was melting away on the horizon, you could see out
and across more clearly, first the buildings of
the boroughs, then, to the north, the monuments of the capital city etching their signa-
ture more sharply at the base of the sky, and,
out toward the sea, the long empty terrain of
the border. The shadows were advancing,
dust fell back to earth beneath pedestrians'
soles, everything huddled against the ground
and the sky took up all the room. I told myself
that I was feeling rather good waiting for my
husband in the evening air, that I would do
well in the future to take some time for myself
like that, and that the bakery must be closed,
my husband must have had to look for an-

other one farther on, and he, too, had stopped
to breathe.

*T*he sun touched the rooftops and the
borough went black against the sky;
the sun was right there, horizontal, gently
warming my face, a redness pressing against
my cheeks. I saw the double outline of the tip
of my nose, going in opposite directions as my
eyes shifted south and north, and the guardrail of eyelashes, very blurry in the light; and
I felt as if I were one big thing, warm and
vibrating, myself. That evening was the last
time in my memory that I succeeded in per-
ceiving myself as whole, full, and collected;
after that I scattered like the galaxies, vaporized out across space like a red giant. The sun
slipped between my eyelids, there was only a
thin line of light left, then it disappeared with
a flash and my nose became a little white mass
set too close beneath my eyes.

The air was cold on my cheeks, and my
hunger was becoming acute. I wanted to break
away from the window and find out what time
it was but I stayed there, waiting a little longer,
not wanting to admit that my husband's delay
was becoming stranger and more objective,
measurable in minutes and quarter hours. I let
anger swell inside me as if it were a last burst

of sunlight I was warming between my hands
so I wouldn't be left alone at my window in the
cold. I fanned my anger, my hunger, I made it
a point of honor not to go and eat a little piece
of cheese, cultivating hunger and anger in order to throw them in my husband's face: who
had held him up in the streets of the borough,
what worthless chatterbox of a neighbor, what
contemptible distraction had slowed him on
the sidewalk to gawk while I was dying of
hunger? My impatiens were losing their color,
a few final petals did their utmost, then gave
up all at once, like that evening's sun, a red
lozenge against a white sky that had simply
dropped to the other side of the Earth. The
swifts were still zigzagging, some of them
skimmed close to my window, their sides blue,
throats ruffled, their bodies no more than a
whistle full of wind, two hollow wings around
a cry.

*T*he air was becoming more and more
palpable. Underlying its balminess was
a shaft of cold like a material quality of silence. The swifts were taking aim at the lady-
bugs on my impatiens, I brought the
flowerpots inside, one of my nightly chores, I
set them there, at my feet, beneath the window. It was important not to leave the window

so that the time I had spent waiting for my husband would be nothing more than a short break to look out at the city, like any house-wife who allows herself a cigarette in the evening before sitting down to dinner with a sigh.

The swifts stopped calling, the sun had fallen too low. Two or three times more their wings gave off a dusting of light, then every-thing turned gray, the air emptied of birds in swirls like a giant bathroom sink. I stayed there alone to float in the evening, on the sky with its soiled edges.

I n the glow of the open refrigerator I cursed my husband. There were two to-matoes and a piece of gruyère; I could make pasta. When he came in, the food would be waiting for him, fully prepared, uncovered, vengeful, a congealed reproach served on cold plates. A last red ray slid across the Formica, the sink grew dim, the dishwashing liquid turned opaque in its anatomical container. I watched the time on the programmable elec-tric oven, I let go of the refrigerator door, I picked up the telephone.

I didn't call the police right away. I called Jacqueline. I didn't say anything to her about my husband's delay, I just wanted

(it was stupid) to know if he wasn't by any
chance at her house. It did me good to hear
Jacqueline, only Jacqueline, and the children's
shouts and the slosh of a bath, Jacqueline's
solidity within the beginning of my anguish,
the volume she filled, her silhouette in space
like a lively swallow. In the world Jacqueline
inhabited, it was impossible just to disappear
like that while going out to get bread. *I'm
busy right now*, she told me, *call me back
later. What are you making for dinner?* I shot
back, and in the return of her impatient voice
I could breathe the aroma of the casserole and
see again the joyful chaos of her apartment,
children covered with boo-boos wreaking
havoc on carpets softer than the ones at my
house. *Just a second, Jacqueline, it wasn't
tonight, was it? The big game on TV? What
big game? The big game the men were going
to watch. What are you talking about?* This
brief exchange over the phone left me suspended in painful midpoint, reassured, certainly, by the virulent presence of my friend
(unaffected by telephone wires or satellite
transmissions, nothing could disintegrate Jacqueline, and her voice on the telephone faith-
fully epitomized her) but also forsaken at the
edge of a very large sea, and I watched Jac-

queline moving away, distractedly waving her hand.

I turned on the television, the eight o'clock news was ending, any moment now, I thought, the announcer would put on a serious face to announce the disappearance of my husband, knocked down by a bus rushing too quickly back to the station, struck by a restaurant delivery boy's moped, crushed to a pulp beneath a taxi taking its last fare home. The streets were empty; the advertisements were already parading by and I could no longer hear any noise outside. I had the strength to switch it off, the voices disappeared, and for the first time that evening I felt myself overwhelmed by a wave of panic. It does not take an hour to buy a baguette, and my husband, always so responsible, would not have left me in the dark about it if by some very strange chance he had stopped to have a drink somewhere.

I set out to make the rounds of the neighborhood in methodical fashion: I walked down the boulevard to the bakery, went across, looked at the sign announcing the hours of operation and peered through the metal shutter. My husband wasn't there. I continued on to the next bakery, a pretentious window display of harvesters against a horizon of wheat and a sign in a retro typeface; my husband never went there. I stood on tiptoe anyway, but the only thing I could smell through the windmill-shaped bars was staleness.

There was another bakery at the intersection, also dark and empty. The streets beyond that were outside of my husband's daily sphere. My heart started hammering—where else to look besides the bakeries? My own powerlessness as I faced the deserted streets made my legs go hollow; my body did away with me to fill up with an alien fluid, like a reservoir of flour or of tears.

I retraced my steps. A movement in the branches or a fluctuation under the streetlight was enough to show me the two of us there, walking through the streets as we had on evenings when our double shadow preceded us and the sky was a magnificent, inexhaustible thing beyond the rooftops. I came out into the plaza, the clock on the borough hall was broken, I let my eyes wander idiotically as if I were going to run across us, sitting side by side next to the fountain, our gazes far away in the sky. I dipped my fingers into the fountain. The lapping surface moved like a net over the crosspieces of the tilework, which seemed to float between two layers of water. In a few minutes, surely, we would be laughing in relief (it was a misunderstanding, a slip in the space-time continuum, a very brief, very benign loss of memory on the part of my husband, who is wandering a hundred meters from me right now. In the sky, two insomniac swifts are laughing as they watch us stumble past each other in the grid of streets, slate and tile, brick and stone). I was still sitting next to the fountain, my consciousness sharpened like a blade but reaching toward nothing at all, a gaping, empty edginess. A liquid mass welled up in my chest, distended below my sternum and tried to spurt from my sides, the slightest movement and I would gush out like a wine barrel. The plaza fell back into place around me, the flagstones floated flat on the ground, the street lamps cut out little cookies of red asphalt. I stood up, very straight. The silence crackled like burning wood. The back of the plaza swayed, and everything trembled as if under the blow of a gong, the air vibrated at ground level. I saw a gleam slip across the facade like a lone silhouette in a reflection.

The fountain behind me started flowing and I came back to myself with a start, a pair of neighbors were approaching, they greeted me. My body remembered on its own, without me. I spoke the words *bonsoir* into the silence and the words folded into themselves like two black wings, I heard the echo of my footsteps.

I knocked at the baker's house. A shutter opened, her face appeared, haloed in blue by the light from the TV. I felt like an idiot. Do you remember, I asked, a rather tall gentleman, wearing dark clothing, who came to buy some bread from you at exactly seven-thirty? The baker considered me in alarm. *As if I had to remember every one of my customers!* she protested. I walked away, pondering her response. I had no desire whatsoever to tell my story, no desire whatsoever to speak the words that my husband had not come home.

I could not picture my husband at another woman's house while I wandered the streets, lost, looking for him, I couldn't picture it not because his fidelity was something I took for granted but because my husband was a consistent man who would never have let me worry about him alone like that: he would have phoned me instead to tell me that on the way to the bakery he had remembered something urgent, gone back to the agency, and would be home very late. At the agency, the phone rang into a void. And yet I saw him, distinctly, painfully, he was there, his back hunched over his computer, his birthday yucca swelling in the thick air, the chair squeaking a little beneath his weight—that always had an erotic effect on me, that stupid chair giving in beneath the tangible weight of my big husband. I pushed the redial button and the ringing started up again, hypnotic, each ring sank a sorcerer's needle into my spine and I squinched my eyes under the effect of a strange, faraway pain.

I pressed my forehead against the window glass, arms dangling, the receiver in my hand. I heard the stipplings of my husband's absence from very far away. The pointless ringing echoed everywhere, on the plaza's flagstones, across the borough to the sea and to the monuments. Drops trickled down beneath my angled forehead and suddenly I understood that it was true, I wasn't dreaming, my husband had not come home after he went out to buy a baguette this evening, and that was what was real and that was what existed. And in the days to come, I would have to experience this shock to the heart again and again, the sudden surge of adrenaline, an electric wave that crashes into the tips of the fingers

13

and paralyzes the throat, freezing the organs
and lingering like a frost in the innermost
bronchioles, the adrenaline that would be, in
the days to come, in my veins and muscles, the
mark of the real, its instrument, its texture.

II

*T*rembling, I sat down on a kitchen stool, one of the bright yellow stools we bought when we moved in, I can see us now arguing about the color: my husband would have preferred a natural wood finish. Sitting in the kitchen, I clutched the feet of the stool below me for dear life, a ridiculous position; and it felt as if my husband were about to come back in a minute to tell me again that we should have bought them in the natural wood finish. My husband was occasionally subject to that type of regret. I saw myself with him in the department store, and reality was that, too: cozy, banal reality with its practical, affordable furniture. I ran my fingers across the table, half paralyzed by the shock of these two realities that were so different, so inexplicably different, my husband's absence and the very present yellow stools. I ran my fingers across the table and it would have been so simple, so normal, to find some crumbs left over from our meal there, the crumbs of reality, a livable reality in which my husband came home with the bread.

*T*he night was entirely black now. I got up. The empty space in my chest was breaking up a little, maybe with the movement, the bizarre weight of that empty space was voided and then returned and settled back into place, precisely centered between my bones, drilled into the hollow of my thorax until I could have spit up blood. My forehead fell back against the window. It was raining now, a damp drizzle that left everything vaporous and glistening, every wall decomposed around its own shape, rooftops blurred, insects pickled in the mist. Then I saw my husband coming back, his steps long and a little unsteady, his coat, his stooped shoulders, his tall silhouette. I ran down the stairs. The street was deserted. I took a few steps in one direction, then the other. I stopped to listen. I saw him farther on, across the street, his thick soles leaving streaks on the wet sidewalk; I ran, he turned his back on me, I called out. A man gazed at me in astonishment. It wasn't my husband. Besides, the coat was nothing at all like his.

I went back upstairs and picked up the telephone, which was like the earliest beginning of a person who would speak to me, like a tiny incipience of my husband. I dialed my mother-in-law's number. My mother-in-law had suddenly fallen ill, the baker had given my husband the news, in his panic he hadn't thought of letting me know, perhaps he was already at her bedside in the hospital. A voice thick with sleep answered the phone. I realized it was starting to get very late. I said my name. There was a click. I pressed redial. I repeated my name in a lively voice, apologizing for the lateness of the hour.

I heard nothing then but a tense breathing, the almost palpable impulse of every nerve cell in the brain, the form that contact between two people in the dark can take, a straining or flickering of memory. At that moment a kind of disengagement occurred between my mother-in-law and me, a slippage that should have made me react, get a grip on myself, speak one of those phrases for which the words are always lacking: not some witty retort, but an impossible, metaphysical phrase, a phrase

that brings something into existence. How
could I tell her that my husband, her son, had
disappeared? Between my mother-in-law and
I at that moment, that very brief moment
ground down by night, a silence passed as
they say angels do. In that silence, I was like a
word that's on the tip of the tongue; my
mother-in-law had an intuition of me (basi-
cally the one she had always had: I existed, I
was her son's wife), an intuition that was
enough, in any case, to make me her daughter-
in-law; somewhere in her there still ticked the
memory of a cascade of blond hair, a sixth-
floor apartment crammed with books, and a
fleeting moment in a borough hall when her
son had said yes to those books and that
blondness.

But I felt the dream fade without being able
to catch hold of it, without being able to speak
the words that would have kept it there between us, would have powerfully allied us. Still
linked from telephone to telephone, our voices
rose through space to ricochet off satellite
panels and bounce back so quickly that I
would have liked for my impossible words to
precede me, to be invented by the telephone
without me and to sound in the void between
the stars until they brought us together once
and for all. In their place I heard, responding

to the uncertain silence on the line, something like the beating of a faltering wing, something that was fleeing and clumsily found a way to take flight.

I fell between the satellites, a free fall into the night, released from weight, released even from my mother-in-law's powerful terrestrial attraction by the modules that attached her to her son. Even so, though no longer able to join together, we were already, both of us, on the other side of the circle of ashes that the living who are yet unscathed place around vampires, harmful things, and bad memories. Into the gaping space that had opened between us, I breathed two words before hanging up: *excusez-moi.*

*D*uring nights of insomnia, when my husband's large drowsing body was like an island in the middle of our immense bed, it could happen that I saw the furniture move or stared so hard into the darkness that I lost myself; then I would burrow close against him (nothing has ever seemed more mysteriously simple, known, and real than my husband's large drowsing body). I turned on all the lights. I dialed the number for emergencies, I waited a long time, making an effort not to feel even more irrationally alone than I actually was, *this is the police department, please stay on the line*. Then a living voice, I was able to explain what was happening to me in very simple words, it had now been five hours since my husband should have come back, the reality was plain, the delay was sufficient. They took my case seriously. They wrote down my name, told me to call back tomorrow if I still had no word, the voice was decent, they insinuated nothing, for the moment they were keeping their statistics on adultery to themselves.

I turned on the TV, very loud, it was a debate between two candidates in the coming elections; I had the stupid feeling that if anything whatsoever were to happen to me (the door bursts open and my husband's abductors bring me his little finger wrapped in newspaper) I could always call for help and the two candidates would rise up as a single man and demand that something be done for me. I walked through the apartment. At the back of the bedroom, I could still hear their voices, they were talking about concrete things, figures, hard facts were what the journalists wanted from them, it did me good. I smiled at the memory of my husband on election mornings, the brave new worlds of our

breakfasts, our splendid moments of self-
congratulation in the kitchen, his bare feet
nervously tapping the base of the stool but his
shoulders squared, my husband who was
going to vote the moment he finished his
coffee, he stood up, I stood up after him, we
went out dressed in fresh, crisp clothes, we
crossed the streets of the borough greeting
all the local people, from no more than the
arrangement of her geraniums my husband
deduced that the lady next door was not going
to vote as we were. He went into the voting
booth and at the very last moment (I'm certain of it, without ever having had any kind of
proof), in a regressive reflex, a kind of old-
fashioned common sense inherited from his
mother came over him: checking to make sure
the curtain was tightly closed and that despite
his height even the topmost wrinkles of his
duplicitous forehead would not betray him
above the curtain rod, my husband, without a
second thought for our exaltations, slipped the
wrong ballot into the envelope and gave a
blank check to the status quo. The blue image
on the TV seemed to overrun its frame and
precipitate in the air, suspended in space like a
shower curtain. I threw myself onto the sofa,
wrapped my arms around a cushion, and
buried my face in it, it smelled of dust and

harshness, I had just had an intuition that we
might never build the world of our breakfasts
together, that perhaps I would vote alone from
now on, in perpetual ignorance of the contents
of his envelope, and that perhaps I would
never again be able to suspect, spy on, and
contradict my traitor of a husband.

*I*n the days and the weeks to come, I
would confirm, with growing lassitude,
that this was to be my way of life from now
on, alternating and painful: my habitual
dreams and memories of a life shared with
someone else reduced to nothing, in steady
salvoes, by the gunpowder of this single physical truth: my husband was gone.

That first night, I managed to discipline
myself enough to go through the motions of
daily life (as if they were capable of bringing
my husband back to me; I shared them with
him alone). I brushed my teeth, trying not to
look at the second brush, the blue one with its
bristles all splayed. Once during a parlor game
I was unable to say what color it was and I was
ashamed, as if this betrayed an inattentiveness
to my husband; in our mutual discomfiture we
thought we had provided our friends with
proof of the poor quality of our love, as if we
had fallen into the kind of trap the police use

22

to detect false marriages. Already on my wedding day, in my understated white suit, the kind you can wear out to dinner once the ribbons have been removed, I had felt suspicious eyes resting on me, not that anyone expected any guarantee of my right to wear that color, our families were no longer at that stage, at least, but it seemed to me that everyone was wondering how a usurper, a bluestocking like me, with my strange conversation, faraway eyes, thin hair, had succeeded in convincing a man as upright, lucid, and financially stable as my husband to take me as his wife, when he could not be unaware (no one was unaware) that I would stay home in lazy pursuit of my studies, doing very little housework, and preparing even fewer delicious meals. My mouth full of toothpaste, I felt a frustrated impulse in the hollow of my muscles to throw myself around his neck and beg his pardon for all my neglect.

I was tempted to turn out the light without having performed my customary inspection of the progress of my wrinkles or even applying my night cream, but two related thoughts stopped me: the thought of my husband, who by all rights would reappear the next day, everything would be back in its place, in an instant of madness he had embarked for the

islands but came swimming back in full pos-
session of his recuperated wits, and the
thought of my own self-esteem, after all, it was
mainly for myself that I worked at making
myself beautiful every night, and every morning, as well.

*W*hen I came out of the bathroom I
felt a little better. But at the sight of
the deserted living room, the television casting
a green light on the carpet (it was a documentary about the Amazon), I wondered again
how to live in this empty apartment, and I no
longer knew, finally, if I was waiting for my
husband or if the wait had become something
else, a general state of being, a malady. I no
longer felt anything but a feverishness, an
aimless tension, the same powerlessness as I
felt in the moments when I willed myself to
understand what brought us together (a
ridiculous question, I know, and one that
certainly did not arise in regard to whatever
lovers I had happened to have, but an inevi-
table question, which I could no more put out
of my mind than the memory of my dead). At
those moments when I expected to grasp my
love for my husband (such as the night before
my wedding, or at the onset of adulterous
thoughts), I waited for an answer that would

burst out of me as an immediate, overwhelm-
ing feeling, yet those were precisely the
moments when I was certain that what people
call feeling, that scattered, daily affection,
would be broken down by the circuits of my
brain; I was expecting sensory proof, but the
question acted as a detergent; my putative
love disappeared under the abrasion of my
neurons and I was left smooth and hard as
enamel. I was entering the regions where you
believe in the one true love, the thunderbolt
to the heart, romantic exaltation; all that I
should necessarily have felt at the mere men-
tion of my husband's name. And then I was in
despair, my heart was too dry, my basic nature
too egotistical, my flanks were barren, my soul
was a cortex, and my husband was a very unfortunate man.

That night, the first night in the seven years
of our life together that I didn't know where
he was, the question of his disappearance left
me even more dazed than the question of my
love. But the analogy saved me from total
panic (from the tolling bell that gave a rhythm
to the increasing abstraction of my wait as it
spiraled tangibly into my chest), for I was
forced to acknowledge the gallingly obvious
fact that the adrenaline shock of his disappearance, the shock I fought back with all my

strength, trying to forget that it would boil up inside me over and over, to pulsate in the tips of my fingers, was the long-awaited proof of my love for him.

I was also saved from hysterical break-down by the near-certainty, toward three o'clock in the morning, that my husband had stage-managed the scenario of his disappearance only to bring me to an awareness of my love, in the sole aim of making a triumphal return as soon as he (in his turn) wielded the proof of my despair, to receive the multiple blows I would not fail to administer, what a jerk, after having abandoned me for how long to the terrors of widowhood.

A new certainty seized me around three-fifteen: my husband was a man devoid of imagination, and in addition extremely kind; even if he was tormented by doubts, he would never have set up this kind of stratagem to extract an admission from me; he would have chosen blackmail over silence. The documentary about the rain forest was still on, the room was awash in green, and in the grip of this new idea that my husband would never have disappeared for me (an idea that was putting me in a very bad mood), I felt the panic returning, pressing me with its cold fingers, my heart bucked madly and once more I was overrun by physical symptoms, the quick pulse, the sweat on my back, the short-ness of breath. A dugout glided across the forest canals, filmed from the surface of the water, people who were clearly frantic tried to maintain an improbable promontory beneath a protective covering of leaves, branches, and lianas that reverberated with monkey screeches and who knows what other horrors, thick brown bubbles burst in the dugout's wake, a dorsal fin sank beneath the surface, and slowly I began to strangle, unable to change the channel, my heart beating, my mouth open, my mind mired in the wait for my husband and in the green veins of the Amazon.

Suddenly, as a helicopter rose straight into the sky over the trees, revealing the path of the river and the tangled mass of its tributaries, suddenly, as I began to breathe again in the wide open sky, I told myself that the whole thing was absurd, that it was obvi-ous and obligatory that by the following night at the very least I would be sleeping with my husband as I had done for seven years without exception, and I went to bed.

*F*airly soon, however, I switched the light back on and decided to make myself a cup of chamomile tea. My chamomile tea drunk, perched on one hip at the edge of the kitchen sink, my eyes lost against my reflection on the window, riddled with streetlights, I had the idea that a moisturizing mask might do the job of calming me down. Where was my husband? I thought of the joke children tell—a sailor asks the captain if something is lost when you know where it is; of course not, says the captain; good, then your pipe isn't lost, it's at the bottom of the sea—where was my husband at that precise moment as I spread a thick green paste across my face, my hair tightly secured by a clip, I took great care outlining the rise of the cheekbones, the contour of eyes and mouth, trying to focus all my attention there; my green face with its huge white eyes was an extraterrestrial, an antediluvian creature of the depths, an outdated model of ghost. I sat down in the living room to let the mask set and turned on the TV again. I wanted to believe that my husband still shared the same space I did, that we were still two fish in the same sea, that a somewhat precise fishing expedition would be all we needed to find ourselves caught in the same net.

I changed channels without watching, I was trying to feel his presence somewhere, in the streets, in the city, on the planet. It should have been possible, it should have been part of our capacity as human beings to make use of telepathy, to feel at a distance our mutual pulsations (or something of that kind). I made a terrible effort to concentrate to the utmost; my brain, exhausted by the wait, rebelled, threatened a migraine, I wanted to believe that if I achieved the correct wavelength I would be able to find my husband again by the mere vibration of my antennae: our marital union itself should have enabled us to communicate like that, and again I felt that my powerlessness was a failure of our bond as a couple, a weakness of my moral fiber.

Then the idea I had wanted to suppress until then came thundering to the surface: I could not succeed in reaching my husband, despite my extreme focus, because he was dead. Under the smashing fist of that idea, at four o'clock in the morning, I found myself sitting in a taxi on a tour of the city's hospitals, culminating at the morgue. The silence of their rosters did not prove he was alive; it proved only that his body had yet to be found.

However, riding in that taxi, whose driver didn't know whether to commiserate, smile at me or ignore me, I arrived at the certainty that notwithstanding my lamentable faculties of concentration, my husband's death, wherever it might have occurred, on land or at sea, would have struck me like lightning. Something in me would have stopped beating, anything else was impossible. I went back to bed.

III

*O*rdinarily my husband's breathing drove away all other nocturnal sounds. I fell asleep in his breathing. It wasn't that my husband snored. But his breathing overflowed into the street, the city, filling up the world and allowing me, despite the darkness, to find a place. I let myself go in his breathing the way I would have let myself go in his arms if he hadn't sweated so much; a tiny quantity of air regularly took the path to my lungs after winding its way down all his long veins. I suppose that the night-dwelling shadows were blocked by the reality of his shoulders and stomach since they passed me by without seeing me or at least without daring to touch me.

*W*hen I first got to know my husband, he had already started his little real estate agency. My husband has always had a talent for business and he was able to profit from the city's expansion into the open territory along the border. I've often been extremely bored as I tried (like a model wife) to listen to my husband, who came home in the evening with his head full of problems, the clients whose qualms had to be overcome with very low prices, the municipality that was blocking the sale of the best lots and had to be convinced by whittling down the profit margin; but I must acknowledge that I've always found him tenacious, tireless, and courageous. These flagrant qualities were undoubtedly what kept the shadows away. But myself, I spent that whole first night without him switching the lamp on, no longer finding any explanation (was it the beams settling, a gust of air, the crackling of the TV as it cooled down, the rustle of feathers in the duvet?) for the outbreaks of noise. Yet I understood perfectly that I was playing into their hands. Entertain the least belief in the presence of shadows and the shadows take strength from that suspicion; their reality gains ground and their presence quickly becomes obvious. Turn-

ing on the light only acknowledges their existence, and so does keeping your eyes open in
the dark. Even when I was a little girl, the certainty that my mother was in the next room
didn't keep me from pitching into the down-
ward spiral, though I never reached the point
of no return, when the shadow attacks. There
are a few simple, if grueling, methods, and
with my husband gone I had to use them that
night more than ever before: taking yourself to
task for your own folly allows you to keep the
shadow down to an embryonic dimension but
demands a strength of character that does not
easily withstand the slow progress of the night;
you can also try to read, doing your best to
avoid anything in a fantastic genre, but even
the flattest realism sometimes has a paradoxi-
cal effect (bored, the imagination wanders),
it's best to keep it simple, a fashion magazine,
old letters that give you something to think
about, even a bloodcurdling horror novel
whose sensationalistic paroxysms ward off
your real fears. On the other hand, playing at
Christmas tree lights, that is, compulsively
switching the lamp on and off, has, as I've
said, the unfortunate result of making the
shadows even denser: they can then retaliate
all the more boldly by stealing the light switch.
And indeed, I groped along the wall in vain (in

the spot where I knew, obviously, that I would
find it), encountering no more than the little
mean teeth of the stucco. More than once I
pulled my arm back and yanked the duvet up
over my nose, barely escaping the clutches of
claws, teeth, suckers. I was just as unable to
get up and head for the door; the shadows
that lurk under the bed make quick work of
encircling your feet with their red-hot talons
the instant you step on the floor, and other
shadows move the walls back, stretching the
room out past the length of your footsteps and
you're found there the next morning, mad,
wandering from room to room without realiz-
ing that day has dawned. As a last resort,
you can simply stay awake with the light on,
waiting for sunrise, but this is undeniably a
total defeat, you're saving yourself by self-
abasement, acknowledging, putting on record,
that you are a child. My husband chased the
shadows away simply by his conviction that
he was an adult.

*D*aybreak alone delivered me from
that painful night, which marks the
beginning of my strange new life. I had fought
so hard against the shadows the whole night,
my reason had done combat with the wolf for
so long that I thought I had entered a new

space-time where I would flicker for the rest of
my life, the zone where the sun would never
again rise, which had already devoured my
husband. But the apartment became imper-
ceptibly gray, then mauve. The sun rose in
back of the building, darkness stayed on in
our rooms while across the way the rooftops
began to shine (the tiles) or to unsheathe
blinding swords of light (the slate) and the
reflected rays penetrated diagonally, a strange,
secondary light. It was very rare for me to
witness a sunrise. At the beginning of our
marriage, I had made some efforts, I got up to
have breakfast with my husband (by the time
my cereal was mushy enough, he was out the
door). And then I got tired of it. His dreams,
when he took the trouble to tell me his dreams,
were always distressingly ordinary. My husband has never known how to escape from
himself in his sleep, he was chatting with a
client, he was infinitely selling an apartment
that always reappeared in his listings (that
was the extreme limit of his imagination), he
sometimes even went out to buy a baguette,
and when he lost his umbrella I launched into
a savage and jeering interpretation that put
him into a fury for the rest of the day.

But that morning, the morning of my new
life, I hadn't closed my eyes all night and

dawn was a novelty as much as a relief (no
doubt the two effects were linked). The streets
were still dark, aquatic, bluish. Without a
breath, without even a rustle, asphyxiated
beneath the closed sky, they became almost
soothing to contemplate. I no longer had the
strength to see my husband's silhouette endlessly reappearing, I was slowly settling into
the rhythm of a longer wait, like a forced con-
valescence. The sky was damp, glimmering at
the edges, beginning to grow brighter from
below. The horizon broke into a delicate net-
work of cracks. Some birds I didn't recognize,
starkly back-lit, tossed and turned in swirling
eddies, rose by circles in a single impulse,
then came swooping down, trying to escape
the light.

My senses were so sharpened by insomnia
that I saw the light creep along the surface of
the walls and slip into the apartment like a
sheet of water. I saw it skim across the carpet,
brightening it from inside (certain foaming
rug cleaners have a comparable effect), making the dust and stale crumbs fluorescent. I
took a step toward the vacuum cleaner and
asked myself, Will my husband, when he
comes home from work this evening at seven-
thirty as usual, once more comment on my
lack of diligence and the lethargy with which I

approach my housekeeping duties? In the (very brief) instant that I gave up on the vacuum cleaner, something like a zooming sensation of freedom came over me.

I was hungry. I had eaten nothing since yesterday's lunch. I opened the refrigerator; in the light of the little bulb the aluminum had exactly the color of the dawn. I felt bizarrely calm (my mind, worn out from incessantly bracing itself, was undoubtedly taking a short, necessary rest), and that helped me endure the sight of the two tomatoes and the remorse, the idea that if I had been a good wife I would have gone downstairs to buy whatever was needed to fill up the refrigerator before my husband came home tired from work, and in that same impulse I would have bought the baguette, and my husband would not have disappeared. Birds were starting to sing, the dawn was progressing; the window frightened me a little now, I had stood there for so long the day before, looking out over my impatiens, I had stood there for so long, without acknowledging my own anxiety, that the tight ball of anguish was going to explode in my face in the fractured brightness of its glass panes.

*W*hen I had made the decision to call another taxi and rifle through the deserted agency, and when I came back empty-handed but hardly reassured, in full awareness that I had just used up the last rational possibility of finding my husband by myself, I presented myself at the police station, signed a statement that would lead to a brief investigation (brief because two hundred people disappear every day in this country) and decided to make myself a cup of coffee, since I certainly wasn't going to sleep anyway.

That day, about nine in the morning, the day after the day my husband disappeared, I sat down in the large designer armchair that I ordered from a catalogue (my husband was against it, a long story), an extremely beautiful and comfortable armchair, in leather, and I tried, cup in hand, having done all that it was in my power to do, to deliver myself if only for a moment from the breathtaking anguish that filled up all the space inside me and seemed to swell even more with every move I made, like a fluid churned up by my own energy. I sat as still as I could and all that anguish seemed to gather up, no longer wanting to tip me over as if I were nothing but a mindless container or one of those toys that bobs right back up, but accumulating into a thick layer. Then I thought I was drowning, heavy and sloshing, in my big armchair, brimming over with my

husband's absence. Where was he? Why
hadn't he come home? Formulating these
questions to myself let in the tiniest bit of air,
following their thread I could breathe a little,
they reminded me why the anguish was there.
The anguish was like the shadows, which
fueled themselves by occupying all of me, I
yielded in response and then they gained
enough strength to feed on themselves, but
first they drained me little by little until I was
used up, gone, and no longer even knew why I
was dismembered and empty like that. And
my husband disappeared entirely. In the same
way that it's hard to make out a given point in
the shadows because the more you focus on it
the more it dissolves on the retina and is lost
in darkness, and you're forced to look slightly
to one side in order to isolate it once more
within the perimeter of your iris and recognize
it, in that same way I had to try to throw the
grip of my anguish off center with these questions, in order not to lose sight of the reason
for it. Then I saw anew the simple, speakable,
and unanswerable truth, almost banal since it
fit into so elementary a sentence: my husband
had disappeared. He had not come home last
night. By stating the terms like that, I could
understand and contain, for a brief instant,
the vampire that was bleeding me there in my

chair; I could make it a declaration and an enigma. Then my understanding clouded over and everything became much more disturbing, entirely new, without syntax, without content, shapeless.

*A*bout nine A.M. that day, after sitting in my chair in a state of apnea, like a hibernating animal, I succeeded in getting to my feet, and picked up our wedding photo from the desk. I wanted to draw from this image, from our smiles, which were a bit forced, constrained by the lens, from the stereotype of my hand on the crook of his arm, a sense of reality, a sense of this past, a sense of ourselves as a couple that could sweep away the extraordinary anguish. But the moment I looked at the photo was the moment when I was forced to admit (only then), after a night without sleep or repose, that my husband had disappeared, that my anguish was justified, limitless, and without any point of reference. The picture had moved. It had blurred. My husband had turned away, as if someone had caught his attention the second the flash went off. My smile was all the more forced, my expression all the more false, for I was gripping him to hold him back, to make him focus his gaze. The lens had seized that moment, that tension in my face, the rumpled fabric at his elbow, and his twisted neck, barely a whiteness into which his profile disappeared. Instead of my husband, I was holding the sleeve of a stiff, new suit, a brown wig. Instead of his awkwardness, his unease with the guests, his rigid face, there was a movement, an escape in shades of black and brown. It was a very beautiful photograph. It was the photograph of his disappearance.

It seemed to me, standing with the photo in my hand, that if I had arrived a few hours sooner I would have been able to hold my husband back; I would have squeezed his arm tighter and averted his sudden swerve. It seemed to me that if I had thought of consulting his image earlier he would have stayed there piously on my arm and the picture would not have moved. I had an impulse to call my mother-in-law and ask her to describe the double portrait that sat on her TV. But I was already beginning to think in terms of economizing my pain. Last night, when I had her at the other end of the line, at the other end of the satellites, in the total emptiness of the night, that was when I should have had the force to hold her back, too, to steer her clear and weep with her; last night when she had an intuition of his disappearance, that gasping intuition whose wings I had heard flapping like a feeble partridge.

I picked up our wedding album and was engulfed in it as in a storm-drenched forest. My husband's face was no longer visible anywhere, he was either gazing into the background or toward the sides of the image, and the eyes of all the guests were staring at me, everyone took their bearings from me; you would have thought I had won a race or that I was the pretext for a human-interest news brief, an innocent village maiden on the arm of an anonymous male, a girl celebrating her first communion at a rather advanced age, the white-robed star of some folkloric event. Soon enough, in the succession of the pages, I'm no more than an artificial, solitary, and forlorn bride, hand still raised toward an absent arm. I turned the pages more and more quickly, trying to precede my husband's disappearance, the tissue rustled between the plates, the corners of the pictures popped out, lopsided, the photos fell in a jumble. I caught the silhouette of a passerby in midflight, a leg stepping off the page, a certain girth, the movement of the shoulders, a lock of hair. I turned the pages back and in the murmur of the paper I perceived a shift, something that was ripping, a breath beneath lips or lashes.

Not knowing what to do with my hands, I cross them clumsily over my little white bag; you would think, as I stand in the middle of the crowd throwing rice, that I was afraid the bag was going to be snatched from me, as if it contained my innermost thoughts. I recognize the look I have in these pictures, it hasn't changed, it's the look I knew I had during the ceremony, an evasive look, we would have preferred a small wedding but my mother-in-law insisted on giving us a big one (a wedding in broad daylight, as if I were eight months pregnant). I try to make a plausible bride, to find the right tone in which to offer around slices of a wedding cake I did not order, cake slicer in hand, in that idiotic picture that already, at the moment it was snapped, embarrassed me in advance; the absence of my husband at my side marks me more than ever as a foreign body.

Turning the final pages, where no one is throwing rice at me anymore and the gazes have become indistinct, even the guests look as if they're wondering what they are doing there. A terrible suspicion came to me: did my husband, from the place where he was while I was present at his disappearance, consider himself henceforth divorced, never married, free of all attachments? Did my husband, from wherever he was hiding, think his wife had never existed? I began to weep over the album, an herbarium of withered moments, the tears soaked into the tissue, which rolled into a pulp beneath my fingers and further gummed the surface of the photos. It rained on my wedding and I was cold in my little white suit, *marriage pluvieux, mariage heureux*, Rainy wedding, happy marriage, someone told me.

It's true that in the end I don't have much proof. We didn't want wedding rings. We didn't want to register anywhere for gifts. We didn't want a dress with all the trimmings or white tie and tails or beribboned children leading the procession. Our only concession to the idea of a real wedding was the day itself.

I looked in the closet and found my little white suit, all the way at the back, a bit yellowed, I don't wear it often anymore; it never looked like a wedding dress, but it never looked like an evening suit either, even after the ribbons were taken off. I slipped it on in front of the bedroom mirror. My breasts and hips fill it out more than they did then, I no longer have the girlish slimness that the photographs attest to. After all, my longest pregnancy lasted nearly six months. I could feel the child moving. Sometimes I still feel it. What remains is the weight I've kept on and the color of the areolas, the areolas of my breasts. Before they were pink. Now they're brown. That is the tangible trace left by pregnancy; not many people know it.

*T*he sun was fully risen, the apartment was bright though no ray of light had entered it directly yet, and the light around me, between our bare walls (my husband liked wallpaper and plants, I liked lacquer and posters: no compromise was objectively possible), was uniformly pearly and gray, like light in an empty fishbowl. In this immobility, in this gel that was setting and becoming almost reassuring in its firmness, I saw a shadow slowly forming. Behind me, I jiggled the telephone receiver to check, stupidly, whether I had in fact hung up (in the same way as I would have flicked the light switch to make sure the light was off, and the shadow would have gone out in its turn; but I had hung up the telephone, and I was far from any light switch). The shadow was barely a shadow: I had (as when I try to make out, by gaps and contrasts, a trace floating in the night) to focus on the trembling of the light at

its perimeter. Looking straight at the shadow
had the effect of concealing it. It was a kind of
densification of space that slowed the effect of
the sun as if through a filter; a thickening of
the air in front of me, to the touch. It moved
slowly, it gave the wind only the slightest pur-
chase, but it did not disintegrate, it was only
wind itself, a little heavier. I turned around to
see if it wasn't my shadow, or the shadow of
some thing; I stretched out my hand but it
didn't move. I stood up slowly so as not to up-
set this new equilibrium in the room, I care-
fully looked slightly to one side of the shadow
in order not to lose sight of it, it was so bright,
so fluctuating in the light; I walked slowly
around it, it was a column of air in the air, a
little more air in that one place, enough to
make weight, shadow, molecules of nitrogen
and oxygen closing ranks, I took one step forward into the center of it, it reassembled
around me and I felt a pressure, a hold, it
disappeared.

I lay down. Through the open door of
the bedroom I saw the growing intensity
of the light in the next room. I kept blinking,
it was as if something had just exploded in
silence and with no accompanying burst of
light, there remained these white, straight,

motionless walls. A ray of light came in, the
first of the day. It slipped under the windowpane and immediately the dust appeared,
demarcated by two lines that were parallel but
moving under the faint pressure of my breath,
an unsuspected thickness in the limpid morning; fading, the matter seemed to disappear
into another place. I began to float from
fatigue, I felt myself rise slightly above the
blankets; I saw the room entirely white and
empty, pierced only by the ray of light, and I
imagined the depths of nuclear lakes from
which all life has disappeared and where the
water, which seems heavier because it is so
clear, rests on a bottom of pulverized sand as
if nothing more could ever come to pass; as if
time had congealed into a single solid block. I
walked across the bottom of the lake and felt
the weight of its calm, its stasis, its whiteness.
The water of nuclear lakes is so sterile that all
imprints disappear and the DNA within your
body dissolves, irradiated, leaving you empty
of even the slightest notch or whorl, all future
lineage erased.

The telephone rang. Answering it required
an effort that was like waking from sleep, I
rose to the surface and gulped for air; everything seemed to recover a kind of half-life, a
movement played through the ray of light.

Someone was talking to me, my mother, who was calling from her office. Hearing her woke me up completely. I thought I might regain contact with normality if she and I resumed our old sport; everything would go back to its place, the kaleidoscope would stabilize on the correct image: me, my husband, my mother-in-law, my mother.

The weakness of my voice alarmed her. I said: *My husband has disappeared*. It was like attempting a chemistry experiment, introducing a foreign element into a body. My mother was silent. I don't know if she was searching for what she should say to me or if, like my mother-in-law a few hours earlier, she had fallen prey to a disturbing precariousness. A foliage began to shiver on the line, my mother let out a deep breath, I felt lianas growing, ferns, arborescences several stories high, wet palm trees broad as an inlet of the sea, *Your husband*, my mother said, and I no longer heard anything but the rustling of a small forest between us, a little copse, sounds of chirping. Her voice seemed to diminish, to shrink like a material body growing tiny and incongruous, a blackhead, hardened wax at the other end of the line as if deep within an ear. I hung up. The game was entirely transformed.

IV

*T*he silence looming after my mother's voice, the phone on its hook, forced me back into the center of my pain, replugging me directly into the outlet from which my anguish flowed; I found myself there, stupefied, the whole day ahead of me to spend in this wait that, the night had already taught me well enough, was a kind of monstrous passivity, the culmination of passivity, or, to be very precise, torture. Another minute would follow this one and I did not know where to draw the strength to survive it. I lay motionless, eyes wide open beneath my eyelids, scanning the ruddy blackness of the skin for the minuscule wrinkles that form networks as large as the capacity for suffering, seeing only phosphenes dancing in my tears, which were slowly thick-

ening at the folds of my eyelids and forming a
kind of wax to keep me from reopening my
eyes, from getting out of there and escaping
the more and more unbearable pressure of my
nervous system, the probable explosion of the
more and more palpably fragmenting nervous
system scattered across the spaces of my
interior. I was lying face up, stretched out flat
on the tangle of sheets, folds of fabric wadded
into the small of my back, taut as a bow; the
jangle of my nerves jerked me awake as soon
as I started to give in, as soon as my body's
defenses were lulled and my muscles began to
relax and my brain slowly let down its guard.
All the accumulated energy sprang onto my
backbone and hurled me to the ceiling, seeking something from me: a monster bristling
with teeth, a giant octopus, its tentacles coiled
in my intestines, which would erupt in any
form, contorted, sucker by sucker in the folds
of my entrails, lodged there, vibrating, biting
down hard on my ovaries, its beak planted in
my uterus, which would rupture in all directions, spiraling out foul gobs of blood, my
stomach ached as if it were about to explode
and I gripped my knees; then, when the
octopus was momentarily mollified, my back
started in, the spinal column planted deep in
me like a sword, skewered through the length

of my flesh with its curving tip digging into
the back of my neck, the medulla oblongata
encased in steel, an iron hand picking at the
occiput, an electric fishing rod pulling strands
of barbed wire from my veins with a rasping
that penetrated to the teeth; and I awoke with
a start. Staying awake was the only option.
I had to get up and pretend, keep moving
forward, indifferent to the needles sticking
into my bone marrow or the pincers fastened
directly onto my Fallopian tubes, I had to
pretend to listen to the radio or to go for a
walk along the beach.

At the corner smoke shop, where for exactly
seven years I had bought nothing but mints, I
asked for two packs of Toujours. The cars
were slivers of gray, the pedestrian crossing
rolled out beneath me like a zebra-skin rug,
placing its fluorescent stripes under each of
my steps, I moved forward through honking
horns and exhaust pipes.

*L*ack of sleep has odd consequences. I
don't know how I made it to the beach.
The shushing of the waves woke me up. My
cigarettes lay unopened beside me, the wind
had gently covered them with a fine molting of
sand that slid over the cellophane as if stirred
by the imperceptible movements of a skin.

The grains rolled against each other just
beneath my eyes, pale yellow against the
bright blue of the logo, they looked like little
toy figures tipped over by a force they were
unaware of, round with stupefaction, very
close, very big, seen under a microscope in a
city overrun by chaos. My face was buried in
sand, my nose turned to the sea, breathing the
spray, and the rest of me was also being pro-
gressively covered over, I blinked under the
attack of grains of sand, the wind blew them
away and brought them back to spangle my
cheeks in gusts that were more and more
enveloping; long, pale streams of sand flowed
along the crease of my hips, little dunes filled
in the hollows of my knees, and my eyelids,
against my will, slowed from the weight of the
sand adhering like pollen to their elytra. I
shook myself off. The sea slapped me full in
the face, a heavy swell in a fracas of spray less
than a meter from me, jolting my neurons with
its violent air. Another anguish was possible, I
felt it rising already, in too much lucidity, in
being there, awake, wide open, another form
of anguish, on the alert, standing face-to-face,
with no way out, a head-on, direct gaze. Sitting with my bottom wedged in sand and my
shoes full of sand, I concentrated, as I used to
when I was little, on the minute distress caused

by the sand that accumulates between the toes
and abrades the nails in silence, above and
below, digging its tiny and very hard marbles
into the soles of your feet. I reached my hand
toward a pack of Toujours, stripped off the
wrapping, the gesture came back on its own,
the lighter was there in the fold of my jeans, as
if it had never left, one hand cupped to break
the wind, head tilted to send the hair waltzing
out of the way, the little wheel scraping against
the stone, the unprotected flame that goes flat
(those innumerable moments of my prenuptial
life, the passerby or the man at the neighbor-
ing table who tries to help you out, your *merci*
muffled between lip and filter, sometimes the
hands touch). Crouched low, my face practically to the ground, a strand of hair sizzling
with a smell of burning, I took a first drag
between my joined hands and stayed like that,
my breathing blocked, as a strange patience
was infused into the blood's rhythm, a painful
and entirely physical confidence spreading out
into my nerve endings. Lungs full, belly taut,
I slowly inhaled with all my muscles, my
shoulders, my neck, trying to take the weight
off my chest, slowly I inhaled the blue smoke,
clarified as if by the suction of a vampire, light
and dancing in the ocean air, the pale blue
smoke of my Toujours.

 he waves were dying down and moving with less force, the shore held the water and the wind in longer, creating large bubbles and saturating stretches of sand that would have pulled at the soles of my shoes with the sound of suction cups if I had risked going any closer. I took a look around me, my head was spinning a little, the tips of my fingers were going numb with nicotine under their sprinkling of sand; my epidermis seemed to have thickened and become less sensitive to the wind and the small, cold prickle of spray. The beach was empty, no one ever comes here, the residents of the capital forget that their city lies on the ocean. Smoke on my lips and tongue, in my throat and at the bottom of my alveoli, I huddled into myself, the sky parading across my pupils like a troop of kites making their way through gaps in the enormity of the clouds.

The stretch of space along the waves is a place where you can give an image to absence, a place that brings a little relief because it is big and empty. The time you spend there watching the waves and the sky above as you unfurl to the horizon with the sea is the only time that absence and duration are, perhaps, and jointly, things that exist. I knew that when

I went home my heart would leap like a tiger
the moment I put the key in the door, I could
already feel within my body a movement
toward home, seeing if a quarter turn was
enough (my husband was there) or if I had to
give two long, full, clicking turns, what mes-
sages were on the answering machine, my
husband, the police, my mother-in-law, the
morgue. I felt within my body an urgency to
leave the beach, where, facing the incompre-
hensible breadth of the sea, I was taking the
measure of my husband's absence and of the
impossible patience I had to aspire to, all
the way to the horizon beyond which the sea
continues to roll, I would have to immensify
myself to the size of that patience in order to
contain the equinoctial tide of his absence.
Nausea swept over me, from smoking in great
lungfuls of the iodized air above the waves,
from burning my fingers on the filter, something was sloshing at the base of my throat,
the murky taste of all the tears forced back, a
seasickness in long viscous algae of muck and
salt that would have to be extracted, filament
by filament, from the Sargasso Sea that had
become my landscape.

I walked along the waves, farther and
farther from the metro station, and
reached the area of the blockhouses from

where you can begin to see the first rows of
mines that extend the border out into the sea.
Ferries were entering and leaving the channel,
a whole bustling to-and-fro: did my husband,
over there in the islands, plan to flee even
farther, did he yearn for other countries? The
week before, a two-ton shark had stupidly
beached itself, firemen were hosing it down all
day to give it some semblance of a sea until it
exhaled its miserable soul in a final, stinking
yawn. Was my husband, at that moment,
being dissolved by gastric juices? The idea
almost made me laugh. The sea, its maw
gaping wide, pounced on the sand and tore
the beach away in great bites to spit it back
out ten yards farther along in unforeseen
meanders. I came within sight of the sea lions,
I was walking faster, my heels struggling
against the yielding sand that sank without
offering any resistance, unpleasantly, just as
the bellies of all those obese sea lions, which
the whole city folklorically comes to feed,
would undoubtedly sink beneath a kick. There
isn't much space for them between the rows
of mines, and their population is ceaselessly
enlarging and increasingly degenerate, I
walked quickly and felt like shouting into the
wind, I hated my husband, I vomited him up
whole, wherever he was, whoever he was with,

let him be damned and go to hell in the gurgling viscera of the first passing shark, in the
total emptiness of the sea full of vile fish and
even viler mollusks. I dropped down to sit on
the ground, crossing through all the sea lions
would require a labyrinthine circumnaviga-
tion of their enormous bellies and repellant
exhalations, I took out a cigarette, a fortress
of bodies mottled with black, rust, and beige
blocked my view like a heap of squashy
bricks, backs, bellies, here and there a patch of
fur added on, tufts of mustache, chests raised
in aggression when another chest exerted itself
to gain a few square meters of sand, skulls that
seemed to have been beaten flat with a ham-
mer and yawns closed off with a snap of the
jaws that offered a few points of reference,
teeth, screws, and gums, in this great grease-
monkey of flesh. The dominant male never let
me out of the corner of his disgusted eye; I
sized up the beast, at least three tons, his coat
stiffened by years of encrusted salt, he wasn't
about to attempt the slightest movement, the
least exertion of his flaunted bulk, I threw a
pebble with everything I had and got him
right between his two large eyes, which the
brute opened a little wider, the information
made its way along his lard-encased synapses,
two neurons succeeded in detaching them-

selves from their bed of fat to set the marbles rolling and I saw the hulking mass, with neither head nor tail now, shift itself toward me like a maggot, the two flippers first, a heave from behind and an undulation beneath the skin, a meter gained as the body falls back. I snickered, rose to my feet and walked away with so much more dignity, square-shouldered biped that I was, not even needing to break into a trot, proud as the little mermaid split in two by her new legs and, like her, scissored with pain.

*T*he rhythm of the walk or the ciga-rette finally defused something in me (a chemical reaction, a thermonuclear fission that was starting up in my core) and the anguish filled me to the brim once again but calmly, in a way, and undivided: the agitation of the nerves wasn't vast enough to occupy the body for long. My husband's image reassembled inside me; not only the image but the mass, the volume, a montgolfier in my throat to make me stretch my neck upward in suffocation but without raising me off the ground, the pull was tearing me in half, feet in the sand but the head like a hydrogen balloon.

I lit another cigarette. Mist was rising in the cold. The air cooled more quickly than the sea,

which smoked with a thick white vapor that
condensed into a fine rain on my cheeks.
Every arching wave, as it broke, expelled as if
between plates of whale baleen a breath of
mingled spray and mist. Bit by bit the sea lions
disappeared. I glimpsed a back swallowed up
by the waves, half a chest that twisted away
before plunging beneath the rest of the body
into the black furnace of the surf. The criss-
cross of moving sea foam that clung to the
shoulders of the swell was further undone at
every new cycle, each intersection of the net-
work growing finer and more diffuse amid
other little pulverized points. That was how I
imagined my brain, subjected to great pressure and vaporized, all its connections undone
little by little, foggy and slack (a frayed piece
of mesh, a mantilla of dust without even the
atoms of its own dispersion), and my mind
was vaporized in turn as it sought to spread
out to the dimensions of what it was lacking,
to embrace the hollow, empty, and volatile
body of my husband. I stood there in front of
the waves, the mist came toward me as the
surf crashed down from the heights of the sea,
my eyes were filling up with white, the sand
would become a single entity, without grains,
fused; then the mist would ebb with the water,
the beach would reappear, I had time to

glimpse a few tattered strips of city, the blinking neon signs on the great towers in the distance; and the mist would come forward
again, still too tightly bound to the water to be
able to do without it and spread out freely, the
mist flowed and ebbed to the precise rhythm
of the surf, outstripping the movement of my
eyelids.

I took off my shoes and followed the line of
the sea's watermark. The sand was threading
thin spirals of ice between my toes, a sea without spring or autumn, only a winter and a
summer that depart without forewarning
in great outpourings of equinox or solstice
depending on how the Earth is tilted. My feet
were sinking in, every wave wanted my skin,
wanted to lay me out beneath it and carry me
away, banging on my head; at each new failure, the exasperated wave left a little sand on
my heels, the better to grip me the next time.

Something very soft came and bumped
against my legs and the sea's breath blew
white in my eyes. I leaned forward, trying to
keep my balance, the crest of the breakers
reached my knees, I stretched out my arms.
The thing had left a long skid mark in the
sand, a railroad track, I thought of my husband's body (my chest gone stiff with the in-
rush of a more scarlet consciousness in my

arteries), but the thing came back, I saw it tumbling at the top of a wave, a little whitish mass, swollen and ravaged, a body delivered up by the water but erased by the mist, I watched as it surged toward me and slid along the surface of the sand, now gently guided by the wave. A gaping red gullet opened out in the middle. It could have been mistaken for a disemboweled child, but it was a young sea lion, its body cut in half by a mine.

*F*arther along, I rubbed sand and water on the spot where the body had touched my leg. I moved forward as quickly as possible, without looking around me, in the now uniform mist. The entrance to the metro appeared in a halo, its arms reaching out to the sky. A young Yuoangui was cooking little sausages beneath it, their aroma was so strange within the dizzying scent of iodine, so terrestrial and everyday, that I rummaged in my pocket to find some coins. I said: *The season hasn't started yet.* The bluish tint of his face was accentuated by the reflection of the mist, I know that in our climates the Yuoangui lack certain ultraviolets that are necessary to their pigments and they sometimes turn pale and die of skin cancers. This Yuoangui didn't look at me, he was looking at the sea, the

white foam threw flashes of light into the
enveloping cotton of the atmosphere and radi-
ant tongues of flame rose suddenly out of the
waves, the bodies of nothing at all struggling
to be born into our three dimensions, trying to
escape from the pulverization of space but
succeeding only in burning out in intuitive
glimmers, rolled and crushed beneath the
disaster of the waves. My chest froze beneath a
vampire's suction, something was depleting
me. *But all the traffic to the islands,* I heard
myself say like someone flinging out a life pre-
server (my voice echoing in the entryway of
the metro), *the traffic out to the islands must
bring a few people your way?* The Yuoangui
didn't even turn his head. I allowed the escala-
tor that continually digs down beneath the
dunes to bear me off, I pitched my sandwich
into the first trash can. The city's strong breath
drew me back into its thronging innards, the
intestines of a seal, the great seal I inhabit, I
glanced back to see a last wave, a last
wretched little corpse of sea foam.

V

*J*acqueline's visit, as I was huddled on
my couch wondering from second to
second how I would live through the evening's
nothingness, had something unreal about it.
My mother had called her (the conniving net-
work of women was beginning to spread its
net around me, to keep me with them, gathering at my shoulders in the same way that right
whales nudge weaker whales with their snouts
to keep them afloat, for the weaker ones might
otherwise let themselves slip down into the
spiraling depths); my mother had called her,
worried, telling her something was wrong, my
mother was sending me my best friend. *What's
going on?* Jacqueline was saying, *your husband has disappeared?* She gave a corrobo-
rating glance around the room. It seemed to

me that void and anguish were oozing from
the stucco's every microstalactite, but Jacqueline considered my walls with aplomb, hands
on her hips, *he's never been crystal clear, your
husband,* and I saw with stupefaction that
beneath her forthright gaze, my husband, in
our wedding photo, was gazing back at her
just as forthrightly, my hypocrite husband,
upright, direct, and forthright on my arm. I
pointed at the frame, Jacqueline picked it up;
with an index finger that feared nothing she
tapped the glass and looked me in the eye,
*your husband, his opinions, this existence you
have, this marriage, and no children, I could
see trouble,* Jacqueline's lips seemed to float
around the words like an ill-fitting garment
but she had that air of certainty that always
makes me doubt. *It is quite possible,* Jacqueline continued (tall and firm before me, my
friend had put into place a painstakingly cali-
brated plan of action, developed a strategy
worthy of a mission into outer space in order
to have her children picked up from day care
and looked after and notify her husband to
put the casserole in the oven so that she could
make an appearance in my neighborhood
after work, I could only be admiringly grate-
ful), *it is quite possible that your husband
has been abducted by the police, the mafia, a*

cartel of foreign powers, his schedule, your
standard of living, his real estate deals, the
border zone is still quite a gamble. That isn't
it, I tried to convey, I was resisting the on-
slaught of the foreign bodies that Jacqueline
has always jabbed into me as if with an electric drill, I braced myself with all the recently
and powerfully iodized marrow in my spine,
she had to be told about the photos, the column of air, the nighttime shadows, the body of
sea foam, the mist over the sea, the Yuoangui
and the sea lions (already, years ago, I would
have had to make her listen to the sound given
off by other spaces), but she would have
thought I was mad, that the right thing, for
my own good, was to have me put away at
once, with the loving consent of my mother.
However, something was happening and there
was nothing for me to do but keep silent and
watch. Jacqueline, standing in front of me,
went on speaking and I seemed to see her
shrink, head and limbs, as if under the effect
of a Jivaro taxidermist, reduced to a tiny
silhouette at the back of the room when she
was three feet from me and I could feel the
virulent wind of her oratorical gesticulations
on my face; and her voice split in two, another
voice within it, sonorous and full of echoes,
answered the first in a harmonious and unin-

terrupted sequence. I sat and gaped at this
astonishing phenomenon like a dog that supposedly understands, as it listens, drooling, to
its master's most vehement speeches, only the
hammering repetition of its name, *blah blah
blah Rex, blah blah blah Rex;* I was sitting on
my hindquarters, mouth open and panting,
fur smoothed down, an almost tangible tail
thumping behind me to the heavy beat of
Jacqueline's words, and I could no longer
make out anything but the recurrence of those
three syllables, *your husband, blah blah blah,
ton mari.* And my husband, *mon mari* in his
turn became two within Jacqueline's cleft
voice, reduced on the one hand to an empty
function and on the other to the real image
that I, me, myself, had of him, but only as a
memory that was, strictly speaking, unavail-
able for display. *That isn't it,* I again succeeded in yipping, but Jacqueline was, as they
say, launched, and nothing could stop her
flight into the farthest corners of the apartment, the walls moved aside at her passage,
the perspective widened, the stucco became
microscopic, and as her voice faded it was her
body that began to take on a dual personality,
a kind of counter-body detached itself from
her like a film so that she was slightly blurred
when seen from the front; it foresaw the

rhetorical movements of her hands and bit
by bit took on an amusing independence, in-
validating with its ridiculous contortions all
that she was taking so much trouble to elabo-
rate upon for me. Still, my expression must
genuinely have evoked the wonderment of a
spaniel, for Jacqueline, dizzied, stopped to
catch her breath. The luminous film hesitated
a second, danced from one foot to the other,
then, throwing me something like a glance,
shrugged the equivalent of shoulders and
fell like a curtain. But I had the time, in the
absence of an answer (for, catching a perhaps
less canine look in my eye, Jacqueline was
already recommencing her consolations), to
take note of one fact. This *ton mari* with which
she punctuated her speech (which I was listen-
ing to in fascination, still drooling copiously
and waiting—for what? a sugar cube, my
walk, someone to pat me with an outstretched
hand?), with this repeated *ton mari*, which
sounded in her mouth like an example of correct grammar, Jacqueline was trying, in a
word, to put herself in my place; she was, I
could see, tensed in this effort to commiserate,
to help me in this new circumstance, to love
me as much as I could be loved; she was, I
could feel, anxious, concerned, sincere even
beyond what I would have imagined; but her

face was oddly strained, she was undoubtedly expending more calories than were necessary on an exercise that certainly demanded energy but was in the final analysis no more than one of the compulsory and most elementary routines of friendship: to support me in affliction (like the whales making an upward motion with their snouts). Beneath these three syllables, *ton mari*, which rang in my ears more and more phonetically (a dental occlusive, a labial occlusive, a lateral liquid—my knowledge of linguistics was returning as quickly as my education had, in the past twenty-four hours, receded to a few random flickerings in my cosmos), beneath these three reiterated and, as far as pronunciation went, perfectly mastered syllables, Jacqueline was refusing with everything she had the hypothesis, grievous to the spirit, of a complete disappearance; Jacqueline was driving my husband back to a distance that was even more frightening than the actual distance at which he was perhaps situated if the—on the whole, perfectly understandable—desire had seized him to confine himself henceforth to this state of existence, vacillating in space, curled up in my memory, flashing on and off in photographs, whispering beneath the waves, and I don't know what else. Something was floating

between Jacqueline and me, something else
was mumbling beneath her words like a
presence of precisely that order, and I could
not see myself explaining to my friend just
then that I would have preferred for her to be
silent and leave a tiny bit of room for the possibility, certainly somewhat surprising but on
the whole still lovable, of my disconcerting
husband.

Jacqueline stopped of her own accord, ill at
ease, and the thing that continued to flitter
around her was taken aback, as if the vibration of her voice had nonetheless instated a
space in the air where the void became habit-
able. I forced myself to give a smile that I
hoped was loving, attentive, and as convincing
as possible, but that must (against my will)
have seemed a physical manifestation as
strange as the coquetries of the Cheshire cat
when Alice sees in the branches only his teeth
and the beginnings of his whiskers, with nothing else around them. Jacqueline went pale
and I thought she was going to start arguing
again, this time in anger (she had other things
to do with her time, she saw little enough of
her husband and children as it was), but her
demonstration was intended only to demand
from me an awareness of the seriousness of
the moment: not only was my husband quite

possibly a spy (a revolutionary, a traitor, a
martyr, an assassin, a hero, a psychopath, the
future patron saint of real estate agents) but
now that he had disappeared, I had no reason
whatsoever to believe he would be returned to
me alive rather than by stinking little morsels
in parcels mailed fourth class (anyway, if I
thought that was so funny it was because I
knew too much about it and my turn would
come soon). My husband, if it was him, had
taken the opportunity to leave the room. In his
place was a parade of astonishing images,
masks, screens, a whole comic-book romance
that finally took him away from me and made
him disappear completely, withdrawn even
deeper into my being and my memory, so deep
that I was overcome with panic at the idea of
losing him entirely and never again, in the
literal sense of the word, seeing him. Something unpleasantly wet rolled down my cheeks
as my chest gave a heave and Jacqueline took
me in her arms.

If we consider our body to be a sequence of
dams (the skin, the dermis, the muscles, the
outer membrane of each organ, the barrier of
the immune system, and whatever it is that
maintains, at each level, the whole structure of
the following level, down to the heart, the
marrow, that which makes us ourselves,

shrinking beneath the accumulated incrusta-
tions, infinitesimal electrons swirling around
the invisible bauble that is the quintessence
of our liquid substance), and if we consider
physical love to break through some of these
dams until it succeeds (and here I venture an
image of ourselves that would undoubtedly
have struck Jacqueline as reckless) in coaxing
the hermit crab out of its shell a tiny bit, to
go with its little elytra or whatever they're
called, feeling its way forward toward the tip
of the antennae of the beloved hermit crab
across the way, then something comparable
happens when a friend—even a friend so
combatively rational that the mere idea of an
evanescent husband gives her dizzying waves
of nausea, even a friend who earnestly attends
useless meetings and sometimes succeeds in
bringing you with her, scolding you for your
unimaginable lack of conscience—yes, something comparable happens when that friend
takes you in her arms. With one hand Jacqueline stroked my hair gently and with the other
she held me against a bosom whose amplitude
(though I've always had trouble accepting it)
far surpasses my own meager cup size. The
dams I spoke of gave way more and more
beneath the surging mass of water that was
me, I let myself be carried gently off, cradled,

broken, knots finally undone, liquid rippled
from me, gushed from my eyes in the most
concrete way, spilling its sweet warmth, pour-
ing out into the slightly flabby arms, the
slightly sagging belly, and the welcoming
breast of my best friend Jacqueline.

When she left I was utterly lost, clutching at
the door on my knees, inert and beside myself
with a feral urge in my belly to howl like a
dog.

I made myself reheat the soup she
brought me and looked out at the street,
which was growing darker, and the sky, which
was more and more opaque, dotted with faint
glimmerings that were overpowered by the
streetlights. Time had not stopped with my
husband's disappearance. If I had to face a
second night without him, who could tell me
that there wouldn't be a third, a fourth, and so
on? Who could promise me that I would not,
going along like that, enter a time that consisted of duration, regularity, norm? A time
that would force the straitjacket of habit onto
my mind and body? I saw, pinned up in front
of me, the faint luminous points of the solitary
nights like so many lightbulbs hanging over
my insomnias, duplicated in the mirror of
their empty sky, night after whole night look-

ing at the sky alone (space like a loosely
woven fabric behind which can be glimpsed,
in stars, something else, daylight, broad daylight, but you strain toward it in vain, the
sheet resists, you suffocate). I put the bowl of
soup to my lips with the physical certainty
that my body would not let anything inside,
my throat shut tight, the opposite of desire;
and I could feel time stretched to its full length
in my veins, its coagulation on the walls and
in the streets. I remembered certain evenings
I'd spent alone, only a few rare evenings, before I met my husband; and other evenings,
from time to time, when he was closing a sale
or prospecting for new business outside the
country: I would start reading a book, drink
coffee, eat chocolate and not bother to cook,
spend hours on the phone with my mother or
Jacqueline. But on this second evening after
my husband's disappearance, there was nothing I could compare to the solitude I saw before me; it did not fall within the sphere of
that benign time when I was still unmarried or
curled up in the conjugal bed, horror novel in
hand, transfixed with fear as I calmly waited
for the latch to click and the door to open; the
solitude I could see before me was palpable,
newly uncrated and harsh to the touch, glacial
and splintery.

"*Buried Alive!*" It was an exercise of the imagination and almost of desire (when, snugly tucked under the duvet with all the lamps lit and the shutters closed against the ever-present possibility of a monstrous face grimacing at me through the window, I would secretly read this kind of book with a feeling of security that was almost as great as when I was in my husband's arms); it was an exercise of the imagination and also of desire: close the eyes, reach out a groping hand and come up against a wall, much too near, it is hard, flat, planed, you try to raise yourself on your elbows and bang your head violently, neck twisted, forehead bleeding, you slide forward but your feet hit against something, and behind you wood again, the top of your skull thuds into it, from shoulders to fingertips you're unable to spread out your arms, the width of the hips is constricted; you must understand that your screams will be in vain, you have nothing more before you now but the utmost extreme of solitude. The coffin in which I saw myself (fallen prey to a sadist, a maniac, a mad scientist, or some scheme in which I was the fall guy) could be plain or lined, could smell of pine, copper, wax, or even, in my moments of intellectual fatigue, of the corpse that preceded me, I could find debris and bones in it; but the point was that I was there, penned in, held in check, detained; the only freedom of movement left me was that which guided my hands between my legs (unless I had already complicated the story with hands that were bound together, and was in terrible contortions to free myself in that narrow box). The touch of my fingers, the infantile movement that comes back at once, a pressure of pulp against pulp, the palm immediately slick, this quick, simple movement, entirely isolated from men, raised me far from duvets and coffins, pulverized me elsewhere, all molecules violently diffracted. I was, when I fell back onto the bed, differently reconstituted; this volatilization of myself had released and consumed all that obstructed the gearwheels of my atoms. When my husband came home he found me fast asleep, oiled and sweet, but grumpy when he tried to wake me. Once in a while, if the book hadn't absorbed me as much, I would hear his footsteps on the stairs, his key in the lock, the soles of his shoes against the carpet, and he would find me propped against a pile of pillows, empty cups on the night table, and sometimes we would make love.

Marie Darrieussecq

 t wasn't the nights of love, gone with
 my husband, that made me sway under
the wholly novel pain of physical absence as I
pushed away my bowl of soup, hardly
touched; it was the memory of those falsely
solitary evenings, the loss of that particular
kind of waiting among books in which the lids
of horrible, snickering coffins slowly rose: the
make-believe death whose very contrast made
the vials of orgasm break open inside me as I
lay wrapped in warm sheets. I knew now that
it was possible to hurl myself against the stuc-
coed walls, leaving shreds of skin against their
bone-white splinters. In the end, the difference between presence and absence was more
abstract, more bearable to the mind, than the
difference, entirely concrete and conceivable,
between a night of false haunting (when the
person who is always there is about to come
back), and a night, my stomach went hollow
at the thought, like those that threatened to be
mine from now on.

   If at least I had been able to feel him somewhere, even far away, even gone forever, even
a secret agent or a maniac or a grave robber,
but to feel him, to feel his existence! The
emptiness around me was setting like a slab of
cement, solidifying and becoming palpable, a

certain quality of air, shadow, and silence, a
certain immobility of the walls and verticality
of the doors and windows. The light fixture we
chose, fake tortoiseshell to match the rattan
furniture and the stiff leaves of the yucca,
hung from the ceiling like a drop about to
burst, a condensation of catastrophe that
weighed down on me and whose very annul-
ment (to turn off the light, plunge into darkness) would unfailingly result in a rain of
monsters and ghosts. The point wasn't my
husband's taste or my own; just the angles
of the furniture, the reflection of the lightbulb,
the blankness of the walls, the hard shine of
the TV, the flat baseboard, the tortoiseshell,
the carpet: the mere presence of objects, the
void to which they gave form. I'm not talking
about the shared memories or connotations
suggested by things; I'm talking about a
solidification of void.

It was a physical, rational process that
operated in accordance with the known laws
of my solar system. I pounded against walls
that were full of the void of my husband as
if against a black painting that would have
explained his absence to me in equations. Void
had sprung up in the place he once filled. The
walls danced in my eyes. The lightbulb
dangled. The windows were elongating. My

muscles were tensing and my belly was going
soft. My nerves were undergoing an internal
traction. Void was emptying me, like a poor
chicken, of my flesh and my thoughts. I felt
liquids draining from beneath my sternum,
but the air around me was perfectly still, indifferent to the puncture; the treatment I was
undergoing was not upsetting the room's equilibrium, was not taking up any space around
me or causing the slightest displacement. A
solid atmosphere lay heavy on my cheeks,
arms, legs; a slowly petrifying layer of ash,
growing thicker all the time, made a cast
around me, enclosed me, stole my fingerprints
in order—once I, in turn, had been dissolved
by gastric juices—to preserve me in a museum
of absences like the hollow bodies of Pompeii.
I was sitting down, eyes fastened on the light
fixture, but I could without knowing it have
been hanging by my feet from the stucco ceiling, head down like a poor vampire that has
drunk its own blood, huddled, dying, and
dumb, in the black animal warmth of its
membranes.

As I try to describe that evening, the
vertigo comes back, the vertigo that
siphoned off my brain, drained it of its thinking molecules and strewed void inside me with

the Coriolis force of madness. I was touching
the precise point to which my being was reduced: dancing in the blackness like a final
phosphene of my unleashed brain, a tiny
spark remained, the consciousness of sharing
with the lightbulb, the overhead fixture, the
felt of the carpeting, and the horizon of the
baseboards a single mode of existence. Being
there like another stalactite in the stucco or
a not very shiny pin pushed into the black
fabric of the sky.

VI

I remember that I found, in the medicine cabinet, the sleeping pills my husband sometimes took; I gulped down three large, round tablets and waited for some semblance of sleep. But I was still prey to this spiral, which was quite literally enervating, my nerves and entrails were stripped bare, jangling outside my empty casing. A dog left by itself barked somewhere in the building, and in the uncertain drift of things the stairwell seemed to take on the depth of a thorax staccatoed with barking. In a certain early phase of sleep you are exposed, naked, to monstrous sensations: if you have even a simple, unfortunate sore throat, you become, all of you, a raw, burning throat, an inside turned out like a glove, a bare, sticky mucous

membrane. I remembered some monkeys
recently arrived at the zoo that I had seen mad
with rage, shaking the bars hard enough to
crunch all the bones in their fingers, scream-
ing with voices long gone, throats racked with
tendons. I was a graft of monkey and dog, no
longer able to arch my back enough to hoist
myself above the chimeras. I fell asleep among
bestial dreams. Was it the dog's perpetual
barking that finally woke me up, or the breath
of my nightmare, its avid, red maw? There are
dawns at which you check to see that your
neck shows no sign of a vampire's visit, the
two little red points, pupils still dilated with
hatred, muscles aching from the struggle. I
splashed my face with cold water, rinsed my
neck and shoulders; I let the water run over
my wrists and its coolness rose through my
veins, the place where you make the cut is also
(along with the temples where the bullet leaves
the hole) the place that best conducts the
warmth or coolness you want. I thought I saw
the night's onslaughts flowing down into the
sink, saw the features of my face melt and dis-
solve, but with a dripping hand I was able,
more or less, to restore a form to my dissipa-
tion. The day was sticking its white tongue out
over the lip of the rooftops; from now on, like
a prisoner, I would have to keep an exact

count, on the wall, of my wait Already I was
straining toward the stairwell, wasn't that my
husband's footsteps coming up, the lock was
about to click, the carpet would whisper (and
would I again spend the day pricking up my
ears at every sound of wood, steel, and felt?).
The dawn was an insult to my lack of sleep,
my eyes blinked in its painful whiteness. A
vampire's cape flapped at every street corner,
the terrified shadows slid beneath porches,
growing thinner and blacker as they ran down
the walls, and I seemed to hear, throughout the
city, rustlings, the sound of fabric stretched
taut by a rush of air, gliding feet on the steps of
churches, cellar doors pulled shut. The phone
rang. I stared even harder at the sky, nails
were being driven into my pupils, pinning me
down on all sides. A female voice, in tears,
asked to speak to my husband, hiccuping
large bubbles of distress. I thought: *bastard*.

But then I recognized it, by a particular
note, an inflection on the second syllable of
the first name, *his* first name, about which I
could do nothing, the name that from among
all others she gave him, my mother-in-law,
who wanted to speak to him at that impossible
hour. To hell with the maternal fiber, her
maternal fiber, set jangling and skewered by a
stake, in skillful torture, all those little fibers

that had given birth, without me, to my husband. A witch's cauldron was boiling around
us; my mother-in-law, I knew, was at that
moment, like me, plunged into that great
boiling cauldron, she was searching for her
son among the bubbles, searching for him
before dissolving in potions of anguish, of
early morning solitude (those gray four
o'clocks when vampires claw at the walls and
are slow to acknowledge the dawn, and when
something stamps its feet and rises with the
sun, turns out the streetlights, sets the metros
in motion, shakes the bakers awake, opens
the seagulls' eyes, unfurls the awnings and
makes people come and drink coffee at a bar,
the same people who will, on their way to
work, dissipate the last wisps of smoke from
the cauldrons by failing to smell it). I would
go see her, I promised, I said it repeatedly as if
to a very old woman who was waiting for help
from anyone, a vague neighbor or the young
lady, such a nice young lady, who helped her
bring her groceries up to the second floor the
other day, go back to sleep, everything's fine,
I'll stop by to see you. It should have been
possible to visit her in a dream and stifle her
premonitions beneath soothing visions, to put
her in contact with what, in any case, I should
have been able to glimpse of her son by forcing

my will and my rusting neurons; but I was
weak to the point of tears, hopelessly limited
by time, space, and anguish, heavy and
sprawled like the sea lions in the swell of the
waves. I forced myself to summon up a vivid
picture of my hand resting on her forehead,
the same hand Jacqueline had rested on me,
but Jacqueline truly has that in her skin, my
forehead subcutaneously in her hand, and also
her children's and maybe her husband's, too.

I went back to my bedroom, which was
still dark and where I knew I would not
sleep, but I wanted to lie down, let my legs,
arms, and chest unknot, my belly grow quiet,
my throat reopen, my lungs expand, my heart
slow down. I thought that if my husband were
to open the door now and calmly take his
shoes off on the carpet I would die of it, of joy,
rage, and frenzy. I groped through the blackness toward the edge of the bed, I moved forward, hands outstretched, prepared to bang
my tibias against the corner of the box spring,
prepared for a while now, for several steps
already, stiff with physical apprehension; I
moved forward more slowly, I reached out
my arms a little farther; not one ray of light
filtered in, the blackness seemed even thicker.
In the absence of the bed, I was now waiting

for the first palpable thing, wall, lamp, window, the first material thing that would deign to place itself in my path. I invented a telescoping arm for myself, the elongated neck of a tortoise; I was a homing device, but minus everything, radar, antennae, scales, ultrasound monitors, and infrared eyes; I felt shoulder, elbow, wrist, and fingers disconnect, boneless. I froze. I was alone in the darkness, I alone in all the city to be deprived of dawn, stupidly shoved down the wolf's gullet while clinging to the iron belief that in my room, too, daylight would have arrived.

Children are told that if they lose their way in the forest they must turn back and go forward, straight ahead, always straight ahead, and they will inevitably find a way out, like explorers in the heinous entrails of the pyramids. I applied the rule, but the number of my steps increased and then surpassed by far the number of steps I had taken coming in, and began, in the darkness, to seem infinite (when you are small and first start to understand the decimal system, you want to count farther and farther, you think you will come to the end; the same thing happens when you look at yourself in two facing mirrors and laugh in terror at seeing yourself multiplied; you are in the process of understanding that you will go

no farther, and indeed your understanding of
your whole life will go no farther, you will do
nothing but glimpse the absence of edges in
the world). It wasn't night, just darkness, and
me there in the midst of it hoping that time
would continue to flow even so, that something would happen, me in the midst of it with
my veins and muscles rapidly scattering into
nothing at all, me there in molecules of flesh
and thought that were dissolving into a cloud
(an expansion as quick as that of the bedroom,
this nebula of a bedroom, as quick as my own
enlargement between more and more uncertain limits). I verified *in vivo* whatever I may
have imagined about the theories of quantum
physics: don't look, don't watch, be silent,
set your consciousness aside, you are no
longer there but the universe, without you, is
acquainted with certain embryonic states,
mists of nonexistent things to which your
gaze would give form; you are the fisherman
beside the sea, or maybe the sea is you, or
maybe you are the potentiality of fish in the
sea, but until the fisherman has snagged it
the fish does not exist. In the bedroom there
remained only motion, motion and darkness.
Build a wall, pierce two holes in it, bombard it
with electrons, and don't look; the electrons
ricochet but a few pass through; now, at a

given moment in time, an electron will pass
through the two holes at once; please take
note: a single electron through two holes at
once. Don't look at the glass on this table;
what cloud of possibility did it exist in, behind
your back, before you reached out an unsus-
pecting hand? It's a common experiment. You
perform it every day. The glass on the table
pirouettes behind your back. The table is
transformed into a haze of table, only to
rematerialize immediately as soon as you
bring your gaze to bear on it, as soon as you
touch it with a finger. Don't try to surprise it:
the speed of light is the energy that condenses
it. It will always have its nice little table shape,
its everyday, ordinary air, whenever, in sudden
frenzy, you drop your newspaper to pounce on
it furiously. You'll know its price, its size,
which tablecloth looks best on it, the sticker
underneath (where it was manufactured, its
weight, the material it's made from: a good
little soldier of a table); but you will not know
it. Yet it all lies within reach of your hand.
Even when named, touched, or crossed
through, ghosts lose none of their power or
indulgence.

I walked across the room, resigned. My husband was necessarily somewhere, vaporous
perhaps and on the verge of exiting the uni-

verse, but necessarily somewhere, leaning over
the edge (whatever edge we must suppose
there is) and watching me; like the dead whose
living know they are still there, disguised by
fog or beneath turning tables, behind doors,
up in the attic rattling their bony feet, in
the kitchen twisting spoons, in the hallway
shaking chains, and the least oafish of them in
a breath of air against the curtains on a perfectly still day. My husband, copying the dead,
was going to give me a sign and return me to
existence; the volatilization of our bedroom
was perhaps already that sign, the sign that he
was keeping watch like a night-light, like the
night-lights in childrens' bedrooms that glow
and open out onto the galaxy. Or else I was
moving through the child's bedroom and
would finally touch a curtain, would open it
and see daylight, the city, shouts echoing out
of the schools, or the complete silence of the
toys. Or else I would run up against something
warm, furry, damp, and sticky in places and
say to myself, if the day finally comes, won't
that be blood you'll see on your fingers? If you
took some scissors and cut open this teddy
bear's stomach, wouldn't you find hot, bluish
entrails beneath the belly button, wouldn't
you plunge your hands into organic juices,
uncoiling viscera? Wouldn't you find a little

heart and, higher up toward the neck, beating
arteries and, higher still, if you forced through
and broke a few bones, little budding teeth
and a tongue ready to speak? Ghosts are
strong, the better to drive you mad, my dear. I
threw the bear as far from me as possible, into
nothing at all. He flew without any sound of
falling, without result, without end.

I might just as well sit down, there was still
ground and weight. It was our stupid carpet,
I recognized the feel of it, the layer of dust
on the surface. I was calm. Time and blood
continued to flow. There was nothing to follow,
nowhere to grope, no distaff to spin with;
furniture, walls, and electric wires had parted
before me like the brambles around the
prince's horse, I would wake up soon.

I can only imagine it now. When I came
back to myself, within myself, when the
molecules of me took back their form (who
was looking at me? from where?), I rubbed
my face hard, remodeled it, it was there, resting on me, a bit of an oily sheen maybe but a
splash of water would again take care of that,
I removed the wax from my eyes, licked away
the threads that were obstructing my mouth,
opened the bedroom door.

VII

The bed was back in its place, the window in its corner, the walls on their charlatan bases. The sun was fully risen; it was going to be a beautiful day. I turned on all the lights. From now on anything was possible, eclipses, poltergeists, the projection of black holes even into private domiciles. I went into the bathroom, checking the door, the little latch that wouldn't close behind me. In the shower I looked at my thighs, stomach, breasts with soap and water flowing over them. I opened the shower curtain, who cared about the water splashing everywhere, I wanted to be able to see the whole bathroom because it's always hard, when you're a little keyed up, to resist the image of a blade silently slitting the fabric and in the same motion smoothly incis-

ing (to begin with) the skin of your lumbar
region, the tip hits home with great finesse, so
sharp you think it's a colder stream of water,
you brush your fingers against it, start adjust-
ing the tap and are astonished by the red-
dened water at your feet, you put your hand
between your legs and stand there, a little
troubled, calculating your twenty-eight days,
then you see the gash and the two torn strips
of the shower curtain. I dried myself off care-
fully, then rummaged for the bottle of almond
oil, I formed the contours of my neck and
shoulders, rounded and tightened the breasts,
flattened out the stomach, bringing it up into
the ribs, smoothed down the insides of the
thighs, hollowed out the small of the back,
massaged the nape of the neck. I tied my hair
up very high, grabbed the vacuum cleaner and
vacuumed everything, the furniture, the light
fixture, the lamps, the yucca, the sofa, the
baseboards, and, obviously, the carpet, all the
little nooks and crannies I never see, when my
husband comes home there won't be a speck
of dust left. I sprinkled all the windows with
ether, an old trick of my mother's, and rubbed
hard until they were spotless, you could pass
right through them. I emptied out yesterday's
soup bowl, washed it and put it away. I
opened the refrigerator to let it air and

sponged out the inside, the ice cube trays, the alveoli for eggs to sit in, the bottle compartment, all the places you never think of. I poured bleach into the crisper, then scrubbed all around me with the floorcloth, the tiles have that beautiful whiteness chlorine gives, even the shine is dissolved. Some bleach splashed onto the living room carpet, there are light spots on it now, I moved the yucca to hide them. I emptied out the last of the bleach into the shower, put our towels in the hamper and in the same burst of energy took the sheets off the bed, the pillowcases, the duvet, making sharp snapping sounds full of blown dust. The freshly risen sun came bursting in through the windowpanes, dust whirled in the hurly-burly of the room, I loaded up the washing machine.

T smoked a cigarette, letting my hair dry at the window. The sun put a slight blur on the painfully bright edges of the rooftops, and the very blue sky stood out in sharp vibration at the angles of the walls, a light haze of warmth was rising, summer perhaps. Peering into a little mirror, I put on my makeup, I would also have to do my nails, to be impeccably groomed for once, and go out. I scrawled a note, *Back in an hour*, and pinned it to the door.

I walked a few meters into the street. A thick coating of wax had solidified over the city, muffling the light; the pigeons flew aimlessly among themselves and looked at me sideways, the walls were tilting and elongated. It wasn't the street I had seen from the window, or rather it was its exact opposite, its continuation at the opposite pole, and yet still my street, a street I walked down every day, the street onto which I opened the front door of the building with an easy motion every day, hand on the doorknob, in or outside the building, on the way out or back home, and me, circulating through the city, tracing out broader or narrower configurations around the little cubicle I occupied, sixth floor, to the left. But the walls stubbornly remained on a diagonal. Facing the playground wall, the leader of the game counts "one," "two," "three," then shouts "freeze!" as he turns around (everyone freezes into a pose like a statue, you mustn't budge, the wild urge to laugh swells in your belly, becomes too great and rises to the eyes, meddles in the tear ducts and jams them, burns, you'll die if you put your foot down, you'll be struck by lightning if

you so much as bat an eyelash, you'll explode
into billions of particles). Who was allowing
me to believe that I myself was the leader of
the game, even as I cast a suspicious eye on
walls and pigeons that were about to burst out
laughing in my face? I turned at street corners
the same way I used to swerve around my
immobile playmates as a little girl, and fright
began creeping through me. The houses were
tall, narrow, contracted with effort. I no longer
had the courage to raise my head. It felt as if
the rooftops were stooping over me, too
steeply pitched, as if the soles of enormous
shoes were going to rip up the foundations and
crush me as if I were vermin. I searched for
space, the park, the plaza at the borough hall,
but the walls were moving, sneaking around
behind my back, hiding their displacements
behind other walls. I found them in front of
me, immobile but creaking, stubborn in their
resistance, bricks arched on their mortar
grooves, concrete suctioning the girders,
shutters clutching at their buhrstone fenestra-
tions. I walked faster, running ahead of their
constructions through an immaculately clean
building site that could easily have been mistaken for a completed project, a grand opening with flowers on the balconies and tight
ranks of cobblestones; but if I ran fast enough

and averted the final tally (turning around
right now, I would surprise them all with a
sudden shout of "freeze!"), then I would see
that it was really the same all over: the sun
was immobilizing only fake walls. I had to
freeze, motionless in my turn, petrified: for I
saw, standing there at the corner in broad
daylight, no more walls, no more street, no
more skyline, no more city; and those blurred
outlines up above, were they still pigeons? The
thing that once rose toward them vertically,
holding steady beneath their perching feet,
finished off by tiles or slate, and pierced, in
the middle heights of the air, by frames that
delimited cubes where people took shelter; the
thing that once took advantage of the laws of
perspective to sink between two obstacles and
flatten out the horizon's creases beneath my
footsteps, pushing back the trees and buildings to make way for me, distributing paving
stones, asphalt, gutters, and curbs with great
precision; the thing that once suddenly ex-
panded to allow certain businesses and even a
brand new supermarket to profit from the
increased space by opening storefronts in it,
going so far as to hollow out a basin in the
middle of a plaza where ducks sometimes
paddled and where the sun came to hang
like a ball: all of it, that quite conciliatory

arrangement of space, had yielded to another
reality and I did not know if that new reality
was prepared to reach an inhabitable form
of agreement with me. Where my building
used to stand there was now a vertical fog,
stretched between me and other fogs, taking
the dimension that remained to it from its
upward thrust alone. These fogs were illuminated in places with patches that were less
dense, reflections that retained the watery
traces of certain angles behind which, in
another degree of thickness, there still moved
a kind of fish, the birds of a disjointed sea,
people, my neighbors, residents of a city of
fog. And if I got up very close, I saw how the
sun made what had once been a building give
birth to millions of particles of wall; this
matter in suspension could, under my face
and fingers, be recomposed in a way that was
a tiny bit more dense, it could level out, accept
a very momentary reassembly into three
dimensions and resemble anew, over a few
cubic centimeters, the beginnings of a house. I
grew aware of the warmth of the sun on my
skin, on the fog of skin that floated in my most
restricted field of vision; I ran my hands over
my face and the sweetness of it was immense,
powdered with the subtlest of cosmetics; I felt
it gently begin to gel, the atoms relaxing into

an epidermis like vapor condensing into mist
on a windowpane. I saw the dual angle of my
nose rise again on the horizon, the tops of my
cheekbones like droplets, the eyelashes a
swinging casement, and the vague archway of
the brows that scumbles the border between
what we see and what we are. Then my attention faltered and it was my turn to etherealize
entirely and mingle with the other fogs. The
sun was evaporating the world and I was
floating. The city was evolving by the laws of
a sublime chemistry in which matter went
directly from solid to gas, bypassing the state
of liquidity to molder bit by bit in a disburse-
ment of mist. Seated at the edge of a fog of
coping wall, in a fog of city, at the approxi-
mate center of a potential plaza, I watched
web-footed fogs that made quite acceptable
ducks floating on water that no longer existed.

The next minute three people had sur-
rounded me to ask, eyes clouded with tender-
ness, if I were pregnant, and I did not manage
to make them run away until, under the
effect of a strange presence of mind (but in my
life I had never been more lucid than in the
minutes that had just overrun me), I calmly
announced that my husband was dead, which
stripped their faces of the angelic smiles that
were promising me paradise: with serious

expressions they set me on my feet, tightly
gripped my hand, and I was able, eyes full of
an exquisite dusting of light, to make my way
alone and in a more or less straight line to the
automatic door of the supermarket. Everyone
drew back as I passed.

*T*he little Yuoangui who had on his
own authority taken over my shopping
cart walked ahead of me, smiling. Thoughts of
meals were coming back to me. A lady in the
refrigerated section was extolling the merits of
a brand of yogurt that displays on the outside
what goes unseen within. The Yuoangui and I
both had a taste and looked at each other,
him still as idiotically blue and me no doubt
still pallid. It takes several years, the lady
explained, periodically, you must eat only this
yogurt for a day or two; it cleans out your
insides, your skin glows, you become strong,
you feel yourself standing tall upon the Earth,
the roots of trees plunge into you and raise
the constituent elements of their leaves up
into broad daylight, rivers sweep along the
minerals you need, grass grows, cows graze,
men manufacture and consume dairy products
such as these, the Milky Way flows through
your veins, you feel the planets revolving inside you, the galaxies reunite at the center of

your abdomen, the macrocosm acts on the
microcosm and time reverses its course. Look,
the lady was saying, and she stretched out the
skin of her cheeks with the palms of her
hands, the blood stopped, her spread-apart
lips smiled at us like those of a clown whose
white makeup is outlined with tears; look, she
was saying: it takes off ten years.

I looked at the little Yuoangui and he
looked back at me, but I don't know if he
saw what I was seeing (if he saw me, ten years
ago, slender and prenuptial, I preferred not to
think about it) or if he saw the symmetrical
opposite of what I was seeing: himself, tiny
and floating in darkness, joined like an
astronaut to a long, twisting cord and solidly
pumping blood, veins and viscera all visible
like an aggregate of eels beating fiercely
beneath an incipient skin, two button eyes
swathed in gauze and already describing the
movements of dreams (the dreams of the
unborn, full of pendulums, rollings and
sloshings, red gleams, liquid tastes, pulsations
and contractions of organs). I bought eighteen
of the yogurts and slipped several into the
Yuoangui's pockets. As we continued on our
circuit (coffee, sugar, and cookies, hiding
between two rows of shelves we stuffed ourselves with creme-filled wafers), we were

slowed by a knot of people around another lady who was extolling something else, nothing that would make a very convincing dinner for my husband, and we stood there for a while, noses in the air, eyes on the neon lights, ears distracted by music and promises. A slight metallic trembling, produced by the Yuoangui's hands on the armature of the shopping cart, gave me to understand that this time I was perhaps not alone in seeing what I was seeing. Something was being born in the hesitant radiance of those neon lights. It flashed to their rhythm, vividly, and made it hard not to blink; but I forced myself to stare fixedly at what was escaping us, to pin down like a large moth this quaking whatever-it-was that was scattering in disorder. The hum of the neon lights was drowning out the music, you could almost believe that the noise was coming not from the expansion of the gas enclosed in those tubes but from the thing that was blurring our vision like that. The young Yuoangui had gone baby blue, he stuffed a last wafer in his mouth and pulled at my arm with the power of a giant squid, the shopping cart made a sound like a cricket, and we moved quickly away.

When we found ourselves in the frozen foods section, the cart full, my shopping

almost finished, the phenomenon occurred
again in the glacial vapor rising from the
freezers with their temperature of eighteen
degrees below zero. The young Yuoangui
was sorry that he was unable to remain in my
presence any longer and waited rather fever-
ishly for me to hand over a bill in exchange
for the cart; in the brief brush of our hands
I saw an unforeseen object crop up, all in
feathers and scales, which I recognized as a
gris-gris of the Great South. I thanked the
Yuoangui from afar as he bolted, then hesitated for a while between ethnographic interest, artistic seduction, and my disgust with
that kind of stupidity, and finally opted for a
reasonable solution: I slipped the amulet
under a bag of peas, to freeze there until the
expiration date. Meanwhile, the phenomenon
was expanding. The freezer gave off a vapor
and in that vapor a gaseous body could be
distinguished, formless and floating, though
endowed with a kind of will, for it stagnated if
I stared hard right there, becoming inchoate
and almost invisible, but if I looked again a
little to one side (either the object feels more
confident and less observed that way, or the
retina, too long impressed with the image,
needs in its own way to breathe elsewhere), it
appeared in full force at the limits of my visual

field. My teeth were chattering, from cold and concentration more than from surprise, I was trying so hard, stamping my feet, to discern it better. The vapor, stinging with crystals, decomposed in the warm air of the store and again became turbid: it was two kinds of mist intermingling as they reinforced or canceled each other out at different spots, fitfully heightening the grayish densification, the circular, spasmodic, and increasingly frequent movement: something was beating above the freezer at eighteen degrees below, and no one seemed to care. Concentrating intently, I managed to open (mentally, I should add) a kind of window, a screen within the screen where a curtain fluttered more slowly, a gentler materialization of something, a new panel of space, slight, fleeting; I stretched out a hand and it caressed my fingers delicately, amorously pressed my palm.

*W*hen I reached the cash register with my cart full to the brim, I discovered on the receipt the checkout clerk handed me that my bank balance indicated I was still solvent, solvent to so startling a degree that I went straight (loading my groceries extravagantly and without a second thought into the trunk of a taxi) to my husband's office.

VIII

My first time through I had left the computer on and the window wide open, and now my husband's office looked as if it were in the same state of gaping abandonment that his file must be in at the police station, and that he himself might be in, lost out there in the stratosphere (I hoped, at least, that he was languishing as much as I was). That was the afternoon when, after checking through his records and discovering I was rich, I began trying to take stock of things, sitting in his chair, breathing the same dusty air he had breathed, handling the mouse still smudged with his fingerprints, my feet on the wastebasket where the remains of his sandwiches were still decomposing, facing the window where I saw what he had seen

every day, the idiotic street and the desultory
pigeons. In the days that followed, though, I
came back here in order to fight off melan-
choly and to participate a little in what had
been his atmosphere; I sometimes answered
the phone, I made appointments for him that
he would not show up for, I filed away advertisements that no one would follow up on, but
it didn't matter since in his absence and in all
simplicity the sales went on, the border zone
continued to be subdivided, the purchases to
increase, and the commissions to fuel my bank
account to a marvelous degree; undoubtedly
none of these operations had any referent outside of cyberspace, but they indicated in a
very real way, beneath the spectral modifica-
tions of the pixels, that perhaps, somewhere,
my husband (or some tutelary spirit) went on
thinking about me. I had occasion to play, at
certain sites, in virtual spaces he had already
passed through since they registered his name;
I had long conversations with various people
in various time zones, none of them people I
would ever see, but they kept me company,
and it was during the interludes, in the
stretches when their linkage of cause and
effect was no longer there, that I began to
write the story of my wait. With a pack of
cigarettes always tucked away in the drawer, I

tried, tapping on the keyboard, to pass the
time like that, to endure, perhaps to clarify my
thoughts, even if I soon began to doubt the
capacity of such a story to take me in that
direction. In fact, the story became two stories,
I didn't write as quickly as I was living, yet this
life of mine was slow. And in the accumulating
lag, which seemed to mimic the temporal dis-
junctions from which I sometimes suffered so
violently (when the next second seems beyond
my grasp, detached from my body: when
night falls, when a cigarette goes out, when
my supernumerary of the moment, eight time
zones away, leaves me to go to work, when I
can't hold out any longer and have to go down
to the bathroom on the ground floor, only to
feel, climbing back up the stairs, the excruci-
ating tide of anguish suddenly crashing down
on me in the opposite direction), in that lag I
recognized the time I was living through better
than if I had been able to write it without the
lag. Instead of laying my experience out flat in
front of me, writing it ricocheted it back to me
like a bullet shot point-blank, charged with
the precise vampirish energy (an antienergy
like the antimatter of a black hole) that my
husband's absence had injected into my veins.
Across this time gap, this rebound, stretched
a net whose hold was initially as brutal as a

harpooning; the wound of adrenaline reopened, either because I was trying to give an
account of it in writing or because it lacerated
me once more with the consciousness (too
vivid not to be ephemeral, as if the mind
secreted its own endorphins) that my husband
had disappeared. It seemed to me then that I
was solidifying on the spot, blood, secretions,
hormones, the impulses of nerves and neurons
all coagulating. What remained of me was
only an empty shell, what I once had been
dissolved in the atmosphere to participate
almost harmoniously in the reality of absence
and void, in a way that became more ethereal
than immobile. In the end, pain will drive the
mind, like the body, to irradiate itself with a
flux that unmakes it, you pass out before the
point of madness, you evaporate and apparently you forget, every woman who has given
birth will tell you this, one hand resting on
the baby carriage. However, the thing that
vibrated in the wide space between writing
and my life, the variegated stratum that I
imagined to be as mobile as a ray of sunlight
laminated at my window, was precisely what
I consisted of: the growing lag between the
story of this disappearance, or rather of its
effects in the negative, and my life was the
same one I felt widening between myself and

my phantom husband, gone much farther
than I into spaces that eluded me.

    *T*he disconnection grew more pro-
nounced and even more real. Was it
that same day or another one that I went to
my mother-in-law's house to try to weave with
her, in the increasingly indistinct city, an idea
of the routes her son and my husband might
have taken? Together we leafed through the
album of his childhood. Everything seemed
normal, unruffled. My mother-in-law was
quivering beside me, turning the pages, wast-
ing away beneath a housecoat she never took
off any more, heavy slippers devouring what
was left to her of bone and ankle. With her
daughter long since departed for another
country, her husband dead, her son disappeared, my mother-in-law wondered what I
was doing there beside her, the likely source of
all her woes, someone who, quite possibly, had
been following her for a long time and setting
off ruptures and catastrophes in her life, evil
eye always upon her. We reached the wedding
album. I wondered, as I turned the pages
where faces I couldn't remember ever having
seen before were framed, where my silhouette,
rarely visible, had the waxy look of a manne-
quin and where my husband plunged a gaze

that was strangely direct, hypnotic, and displaced into the lens (as if whatever he was
staring at were always behind me looking at
him), I wondered what my mother's album
would look like now, whether it was the exact
symmetrical complement of the one I was
looking at there, and whether, by putting
them together, a complete and smiling wedding album could be obtained. My mother-in-
law was shaking beside me like a leaf left to
blow in the wind, I didn't dare look at her
directly, it felt to me as if her face were carried
off by a gust at every moment, her body
twisted by flurries; out of the corner of my eye,
I thought I saw her housecoat billow up over
her white flesh and reveal her breasts, her
belly, the skin of her arms unfurling in ripples.
Of the face, seen from the side, I recognized
nothing, the cheeks drawn, the eyes sunken,
and the rest crunched underfoot like a whirl-
wind of leaves, a vegetal flesh, veins and pigments crumpled up and trampled. *It was a
beautiful wedding*, I heard; and I had an urge
to look at her mouth, that compost mouth
from which words seemed to issue, among
other cracks, other holes full of dead leaves;
but I leapt at the branch that was held out to
me and the two of us found ourselves there,
singing into the wind like poor titmice left

behind by the migrating flock, both of us trying to recognize beneath the puffed-up feathers of the other an allegedly familiar bird.

Finally my mother-in-law got up to make coffee and I was alone with the photos, the furniture, the curtains, the mats from her vacations in the islands, the masks from her Yuoangui period, trying again to find, blindly and without my husband, some point of reference for myself here, hemmed in by objects whose dusty surfaces I knew by heart but that remained alien to me. When my mother-in-law, returning with two cups, saw me in her living room, I read on her somewhat reconstituted face that she was again in control of the meaning of this visit, but as she sat down on the Yuoangui leather ottoman, with the well-coordinated gestures of her fully mastered role, a wave began to undulate beneath her face once again, her eyes drifted away, something was zigzagging in her gaze and seemed to buzz at her ears; I thought that at any moment she would stand up and flail her arms furiously as if to be rid of an insect. I drank my coffee fast. Finally her eyes focused on me, she must have noticed my hurry, for she held out her hand with a curious gesture, as soothing as it was polite; and in response to my

little scraps of speech (*two sugars, please, the
lovely cups, your last trip to the islands*), she
seemed relieved to be able (very briefly) to
gather herself up into a usable, acceptable,
bankable form for this surprise guest who pre-
tended to know her son so well. It was my
mother who, on an entirely personal impulse,
had expressed to her, over the telephone, this
disappearance of which we did not know how
to speak; my well-meaning mother, capable of
decisions as sincere as they were devastating,
and whom my mother-in-law spoke of as *your
mother*, designating beneath this apparently
usual term the phenomenal entity come to
pulverize whatever solidity was left in her. In
the looseness of her gaze I thought I discerned
the traces of neuroleptics no doubt hastily pre-
scribed by her generalist as a putty to fill in
any cracks in the barriers of her reason; but I
also recognized the mark that the assault of a
ghost leaves in the eye, that incapacity to focus
the gaze (out of fear or out of desire to see it
coming back everywhere like the phosphenes
that still dance on the retina at night when the
lamp has been switched off). What had she
done wrong, what mission had she failed in,
what stage had she neglected, what wounding
word had she allowed herself, and what loving
word had she failed to speak, he was unruly,

mischievous, but so kind, sitting across from my mother-in-law I watched the thing that was dancing there beneath her lips and in her gaze, the thing that made her abruptly throw her head back and gasp for air: it was our shared fault, our duo sung on the branch, we had not known how to keep her son and my husband.

I succeeded in getting through to my mother over the phone, between two meetings and two rounds of I don't know what sport, and we arranged to meet after she left work and go to the hammam. Jacqueline had called me again the day before, someone had to be responsible, nothing happens without a reason: my friend accused me of inertia and fatalism. She declared herself ready, her children in day care and her husband in the kitchen, to take things into her own hands, knock on doors, she knew someone who could recommend that the case be reopened. Clearly I owed it to myself to act before she, like my mother, triggered operations that might be useful but were hazardous; for Jacqueline (Jacqueline, my matron of honor, she who, beneath the popping flashbulbs and amid the fragrance of roses, signed the certificates), with all her reiteration of *your husband* mani-

fested no more than an apparently secondary
concern to replace a face on the referent of
that term whose disappearance seemed to
have left her with no more than a vague
memory of an entity who, without ever giving
me a child, had nevertheless lived with me for
a certain period, and whom she had, when it
came down to it, not known well, absorbed as
she was in activities that had nothing to do
with him. Now in my opinion (but how to con-
fess this?), it was important not to stir up too
much dust around this disappearance; it was
necessary to let things come as they may, to let
the air settle; my vision would clear, the knots
would come undone, the panicked magneti-
zations would let up: it was necessary to be
patient and wait, as in the powerlessness of
amnesia when, after a period of rest, the fog
starts to break up; at the sight of some slight,
trivial thing a memory emerges; at a cross-
roads, a junction, something comes back.

I walked, the streets were muddled, damp,
autumnal; it took an effort to remember that it
was spring, the seasons seemed to break
through their contour of days, mingling their
tendencies until the sun rose and set on a me-
teorology in emulsion which recapitulated the
weather in twenty-four-hour loops. I could
hear my footsteps from very far away, muffled

by the puddles and splashes, reverberating
beneath the lowering sky; someone was playing at making his heels ring out to my rhythm,
hiding at the street corners and melting into
the echoes. The walls were vibrating, sound
waves were materializing in columns of
shadow at the far end of the avenues, rising
along the walls to be stifled by the clouds; the
clamorous streets led only to rims of translucent sand and endlessly made me bear off on a
diagonal. I saw myself without succeeding in
joining myself: a small figure, in color, walking obliviously through streets carved out in
even rows at the bottom of a plastic bubble
that soon, in inconsequential upheaval, would
witness eddies of snow swirling up, shaken by
the enormous hand of a tourist: and I was
also, as I opened my umbrella and stretched
out my hand beneath the hesitant sky, one of
those dolls made of an odd opalescent, pasty
material that turns red when the weather is
fair and blue when it rains, and that passes
through other strange colors in between. If
someone somewhere was watching me and
still thinking about me, then did I still have a
little more existence than a souvenir placed on
a shelf, abandoned to time between the shell-
encrusted dancing girl, the carved nut from
the islands, and the Yuoangui gris-gris?

Not too well, I answered my mother, who
was concerned about my papier-mâché
cheeks. *Me neither,* she added in the same
breath, leading me to her car, and as she was
backing up she summarized for me her defini-
tive contempt for this life, this career, these
men, her mind was made up, she had reserved
her spot on a boat. At the hammam, my
mother scrubbed herself with an exfoliating
glove, sweating with indignation and plans,
she'd had enough, the weather was unhealthy,
the space was constricted, the city stifling, the
office a cesspool, her colleagues stuck in a rut,
the forecasts too depressing, the waves too
violent, and I felt myself drifting to sleep in
the suspicion or childish dream, which came
rising through the vapor, that my mother was
leaving simply to rejoin—twenty years after
their divorce—my father. *Massage?* a thickset
Yuoangui woman in her sixties was asking.
Head between my arms, I gave myself over to
it entirely, flat on my belly on a towel slick
with almond oil, and I saw, over my forearm,
in a mist of hairs and chafed skin, through
galaxies of suspended droplets, my mother
smearing a thick green paste over her body,
mother and daughter alike we were great ad-
vocates of the mud pack. Her body was outlined against the light from the stained-glass

windows, sculpted by a crust of green earth, fifty years and the prenuptial grace of a fruit tree, five green shoots were tickling me now. I closed my eyes beneath the Yuoangui woman's grip, my loins open, my thoracic cage outspread as if the ribs, separated from the spine and forced toward the exterior, had made the sternum spurt out along with everything that was crushed beneath it, my stomach set free, my abandoned thighs, the half-open mouth, heavy and dismembered, the soggy organs, the mute brain.

*W*hen I reopened my eyes, the Yuoangui's hands had become supple and dancing, they grabbed at the fleshy parts of my body in little rapid touches, I was lying beneath a rain shower and felt myself rising, rising: my shoulders, winged with ten fingers, swept me up toward the vault to take shelter, the cupolas kept me separate from the city; and I felt as if I were going to flit about aimlessly against the dripping stained glass, awkward and limp, then embrace the ceiling and fall back in droplets on the other women, oiling them pore by pore and flowing into their bathwater. My mother was returning from ten showers at different temperatures, washed, rubbed down, exfoliated, and red; but I

couldn't look at her for long, the Yuoangui
had wedged me into the deep channel of her
breasts to dismantle my vertebrae one by one.
I heard cracking and gurgling, I gasped for air,
my body was spilling out behind me and my
synergies were undone, I was blind, melted,
my nose buried above a sex that smelled of
almond, as did all the folds there. *Anyway,
they certainly know how to live,* my mother
was saying as she drank the traditional hot
chocolate while, wrapped in a bathrobe, I
tried to reorganize my molecules, wherever it
was she was going (I hadn't yet had the courage to ask for precise information), in that
hand-picked world where she was counting on
finding security, repose, and even love, there
were very few Yuoangui (headshrinkers, man-
eaters, child stealers, wizards, polluters of
rivers): *Maman,* I said (which was sometimes
enough). But my mother, when I was in her
presence or even on the phone with her, exer-
cised her power over me in a way that (for
lack of a more reassuring explanation, which
in its very reassurance would be inadequate to
the demented force of the phenomenon) could
only be supernatural. Everything I had
achieved at the cost of so prolonged an effort
of approach and understanding (including the
surgically detached reality of absence); every-

thing that, by long struggle, I had gained
against what my family called good thinking
and common sense, taste and temperament,
intelligence and law, strength and temporal
duration (I who knew that my guts were being
ripped out every day as the price of a true
vision of reality); all my efforts, the doublets
that were mine alone, my own federative cou-
plets, were instantly aborted by my mother's
presence. After an hour and a half with her, I
was six years old; it's simple enough to calcu-
late that I lost about a year every five minutes,
which at that rate barred me absolutely, out of
fear of annihilation or fetal senility, from re-
maining in her company for more than two
hours. As she was putting the car into first
gear, I saw my husband coming out of the
hammam, the two large swinging doors puls-
ing steam around him, he pulled up his coat
collar and prepared to confront the anachro-
nistic cold outside, all at once the door swallowed him back up in a sneeze of mist, *stop*! I
cried to my mother, but in answer to my pleas
she assured me I was talking nonsense, it
wasn't a mixed day, the men were tomorrow.

    I couldn't escape from the car in time
and found myself, utterly distraught and
enfeebled, trotting after her on the beach (my

mother, the only human being I know who is
not irresistibly drawn, after a hammam and a
hot chocolate, by the idea of immediately bur-
rowing beneath her duvet). Stretching out her
arms and transforming herself into a seagull,
she spoke to me of her desires, her loves, of
chance, which does not exist, and I, ready for
anything, waited for her little song and dance
on how all men are the same when, turning
toward me, she said, full of a sudden and disturbing solicitude, that it was time, now, for
me to remake my life: was I just going to keep
waiting, like a sailor's widow, perched at the
edge of a cliff with my coif blowing in the
wind, for my husband to deign to come back,
she certainly hadn't raised me like that, nor
had she intended for me to marry so young,
and none of what had happened was particu-
larly surprising. *Maman*, I said. But her
speech was not what wore on me most. I was
unable to immobilize her image within my
field of vision; I didn't recognize her. She was
in the process of explaining to me, in a tone
full of rhythmic emphasis for the ear, that
even if she were to depart for the opposite end
of the earth, I wouldn't care in the least (an
elegy that in itself was nothing remarkable, no
more than a variation on our interminable
dialogue), and I was still making an enormous

effort to stabilize her beneath my eyes. She
was shrinking; I knew the effects of fatigue on
the eyesight, and yet it was an objective fact
that she was shriveling into the background,
as Jacqueline had done some time before; certainly I could have—if the contact wouldn't
have made both of us jump—touched her
with my finger, but I really saw another person
condensing before me, a person who was
reedy, crumpled, and (in the elementary sense
of the term) less solid: a kind of concentrate of
mother, a maternal liqueur congealed and
quivering in a little bottle, whose shrill voice
would have won a smile from me if I hadn't
been shivering with sadness. I could have
picked her up in the hollow of my hand and
shut her in a box ornamented with shells, or
trapped her beneath a plastic bubble to make
snow fall and stir up flurries in my turn. It had
nothing to do with her departure (that idea
remained secondary, unprecedented but fore-
seeable, my mother had accustomed me to
this kind of hairpin turn, abrupt shift of view,
categorical decision that had made of her life
and mine, until my husband's intervention, an
alarming lace with more holes than thread)
but with the crucifying energy that seemed to
pulsate from her like the last rays of those
stars whose extreme density has reached its

final stage and whose death sinks a black hole
into the universe. Her voice reached me from
very far away, without immediate effect, without opinions that could bother me now, vora-
cious and singing but as if emitted by one or
another of the sea lions who were encamped
nearby (a sea lion whose joints creak with
stiffness but who still wriggles its flippers a
little in order to mingle, in the newborn waves,
with the younger ones who will drown it).
Maman, I said again, but as the beginning of a
phrase that did not come. My mother returned
to her grievances with respect to my extraordinary filial indifference, did I or did I not want
to know her new address, when she was leaving, the name of the boat, was I at all aware
of the disturbing atmosphere that was setting
in here, the inertia, the gloom, and worse?
Maman, I said, and heard myself blurting out
my sorrow over my father, which was certainly
the stupidest possible move in that situation,
but which summed up fairly well the state of
sad rage I was in. But my mother had no in-
tention of answering. She looked out at the
sea, and it was difficult for me to know if she
was rereading her past there or considering
her future. She no longer saw me, while I saw
her, standing up very straight, a slender black
stripe against the uniform whiteness of the

horizon, her loose, falsely brunette hair mingling with the gray of the sky. Numerous seagulls cackled above our heads and adroitly released their droppings, widening their oval flight in loops that brought back a stench of garbage. The waves occasionally drowned out their cries, saturating the enormity of space for a second and consoling us by their vastness, as if our brains themselves were no more, in that brief respite, than the ephemeral, thunderous sound of a breaking wave. It has always been difficult for me to assess the degree of relative oblivion, anesthesia, or dumbfoundedness out of which my mother, orphaned from her husband, had decided that tomorrow will be another day, to halt the cursor of her pain; but I perceived all at once, watching my mother watch the waves, that as far as my husband, my future, my dead children, and my adult life went, she was henceforth as little concerned with putting herself in my place as I had been with putting myself in hers.

IX

*M*y mother gave a going-away party
for herself and invited me to come
with anyone I wanted, which I took as encour-
agement to sit alone in outdoor cafés, take
walks with a lost and come-hither look about
me, cultivate the company of old friends, run
an advertisement, what do I know; I called
Jacqueline to my rescue (Jacqueline, my
unbearable, inestimable friend, the only
person I could really count on, with her blind
obstinacy toward everything she has ever
deemed solid: the aspect of reality that dove-
tails with neurons that are cubical). I soon
began to feel very bad. It was a dinner with
a theme; we were celebrating my mother's
departure, in other words we were politely
pretending to expect from this ostensibly

joyous gathering an impossible consolation;
still, as we drank our aperitifs, I wasn't far
from being moved. My petite mother, tricked
out to best advantage, really pretty, was re-
ceiving gifts and distributing kisses, wearing a
new dress that was ahead of its time, guiding
along the conversation, offering drinks, still a
little red from a peel-off mask she must have
quickly applied an hour before the guests arrived; and the idea of her departure suddenly
comforted me so greatly that I could have
melted into tears of relief, touched as I was at
seeing her inflict on me for the last time the
spectacle of dancing bounciness that had
been curdling my brains for twenty-five years.
But at certain moments another underlying
theme also made itself felt. Everyone knew the
hostess's son-in-law had disappeared. Indeed,
out of the goodness of her heart, my mother
had also invited my mother-in-law, which
further underscored the unvoiced theme. My
mother-in-law, overwhelmed and polite, be-
haved exactly as I should have: trying in vain
to participate in the festivities, her hand
trembled beneath her champagne glass, her
eyes shone too brightly at the corners of red-
dened lids, she gave distracted answers, she
was just right, upsetting, harmoniously distraught. I was sitting in a corner of a sofa,

Jacqueline never took her eyes off me, and I saw in advance, very distinctly (like a young witch who has yet to fully master her gift, which sends her into convulsions at the very worst moments), what would soon be occupying this decor: my mother, her friends, her colleagues, and my mother-in-law all strewn across the blood-soaked carpet to the screams of Jacqueline, spared by a last burst of goodness on my part. My mother was whispering into the neck of one of the guests, no doubt speaking of me; her blue silicone dress conformed very precisely to the outline of her body and complemented my mother-in-law's ambiguous mourning in so exquisitely, so elegantly fluid a way that the whole room was sloshing with the emulsion of their presence like an illuminated aquarium where two eels dance minuets among the bubbles. My mother's dress, in and of itself, would have been enough to hold everyone's attention. I'm not saying my mother was dressed in a way that was too brazen or too explicitly sexual for her age; but if she so much as batted an eyelash, gleams of light sheared across her dress: an ice cube seemed to be melting everywhere on the silicone, making it look wet, iridescent, and transparent; my mother's breasts, hips, and stomach shrank back, shivering, at its touch. I saw (we are not responsible for the good taste of our visions) the room's carpets slowly parting to reveal a turquoise, iceberg-studded sea into which my mother would plunge beneath our flabbergasted eyes, and we all perceived, through the garment's scales, the curve of a mermaid's tail that would freeze us in our tracks. *Where the hell did you get that dress?* I slipped into my mother's triumphant ear; but apparently she was not about to pay any attention to me that evening. I began paddling about among the other fish; the whole room was moving at once, and far from me, I changed direction, heart uncertain, under the rising nausea of an indoor seasickness. Jacqueline was overseeing me like a cork. I took flight.

*W*alking through the streets and feeling the sun beneath my feet, the moon and stars above me, the fresh air filling up my lungs, I succeeded in reestablishing the walls on their solid and upright foundations. What pained me wasn't so much that I had been transformed into a creature of the deepest depths (those translucent little crawly things that are reddish, squishy, and somewhat disgusting beneath the searchlights of bathyscaphes), but to see and take note that,

as far as the rest of the clan went, the only
feeling aroused by my husband's disappearance (and the same went for mollusks of the
abysses) was embarrassment, and that henceforth they would circumvent me from afar
with small, prudent thrusts of the flipper,
while pretending to take pleasure in the silence
of the depths. If at least, my voice fittingly
broken, my eyes on the edge of the void, I
had been able to notify my world of a day of
burial, to run my "no flowers by request" in
the newspaper; if at least I had been able, like
my mother-in-law, to suggest that the fault lay
elsewhere, shift the predicament onto someone
else and flaunt a haggard, isolated, estranged
mourning. I had to go back and scream out
my husband's absence, crush the cervical
cartilage of the guests with it.

 *T*urning on my heel, I saw the street
turned inside out, this street of private
bungalows bordering the sea, not really a borough, not really a summer resort, a hateful
street with pine trees among the street lamps
(me as a kid, the street's silence, the silhouette
of rooftops at a distance from each other, the
trees, stiff and black like mummies, and then
down the little alley to the door and ring,
quickly, for her to open: before a thin finger,

like something sawed from an old root, poked
into my back—and if I turned around, I
signed my death warrant). Two bedrooms, one
for her, one for me, and the large central room
with picture windows in which the guests were
now mingling. As I moved forward, I heard
the folderols and laughter growing louder
while the ocean's breathing faded, seeming to
deepen beneath me as if the gravity of the sea
were penetrating the ground in vibrations: an
energy you absorb with a feeling of intuition
until the moment you touch an element of
another universe and are struck by lightning
(as when two opposing certainties are present
in the body and discharge their irreconcilable
betwixt and between in adrenaline). The
inverse of the street was like a sudden rise of
the sea, a night of flooding; I saw a negative
of a street, like a glove turned inside out: I
walked at the bottom of the ocean beside
stripped walls, corroded gates, cars covered
with mossy leprosy, gardens infested with
octopuses, pine trees encrusted with vampire
shells (their sap sucked away, their prayerful
branches forming reefs); to navigate above
this housing development, you would have
had to be well acquainted with the shoals of its
labyrinth, you would have to hear the rudder
scraping lightly against the rooftops, the keel

grating in its track of drainpipes. But my footsteps were light, unflagging and quick, the
water was ferrying me along; the house slid
toward me (my childhood home, slashed with
light like a boat with its stem torn away, and
breathing through the snorkel of its chim-
neys). The giant air bubble of the main room
gave off a green glow, it was an aquarium in
reverse and I was the shark, the killer whale,
the jaws; propelled by my fin, I prowled in the
garden among sargasso, mutant cabbages, sea
carrots, protozoa with their countless flagella,
and hermit crabs, no longer distinguishing
between outside and in; I was going to shatter
the windows in a devastation of water, teeth,
and screams. I saw Jacqueline, her nose
pressed against the window like a little girl,
two round nostrils in an aureole, I saw all the
people who were breathing in there, bathed in
light that was rapidly dissolving beneath the
shadow of the pines, all those people who were
moving in silence in the gaseous thickness of
the room and who endured without a pang, in
the perpetual, even glide of figures moving on
cushions of air, my husband's absence. I had
stopped against a tree trunk, out of breath,
not knowing what to do. The pine tree above
me gave little cries, its branches rubbed
against each other, the moon caught in the

grill of the needles. The solitary pleasure of
the pine tree in the breeze, the tra-la-la of the
music through the windowpanes, the low tide
in my chest, that was all I understood. Someone needed to come, take my hand, speak to
me, tell me to go in.

*W*e sat down around the table. No one
appeared to have noticed my absence
though I thought I could read in the sullen
eyes of certain guests that they had been waiting for me. While the first course was passed
around, Jacqueline was whispering in my ear,
my mother was going away, perhaps for a very
long time, couldn't I make an effort to say
something nice to her, or even help her, as the
daughter of the household, and, who knows,
take advantage of this last time with her in
who knew how long to get a little closer to
her? Jacqueline promised to do whatever she
could to give the signal for the guests to depart
and leave us alone together. I busied myself
separating my bit of fish from its aspic and
avoided looking at Jacqueline, I sensed that
she was smiling at me in a tenderly encourag-
ing way, just the way she must look at her
children when, terrorized, they struggle to
decipher their cello music, force down the
broccoli omelette, or find the solution, jump-

ing up and down in panic, to the educational
game. Everything was starting to pitch and
toss again as if beneath a swell of air, and it
seemed, had I been able to look through the
main room's picture windows, that the tide
outside had done its work, for the raw scent
of iodine was finding its way into the room.
Rising to my feet in the middle of the meal,
throwing the curtains wide open, I would have
unveiled the immensity of the disaster to the
guests, the garden churned up by waves and
dismembered by ebbing water, flayed rock
between puddles of seawater, the house giving
birth to its foundation; and the guests would
go out with slow steps and sit down on the
fallen pines and raise their eyes to a sky cum-
bered with tornadoes that would bring the
breakers back down upon us. Yet conversation
carried on; for several minutes now my mother
in her trail-blazing dress had been trying to
steer it away from an overly polemical trajec-
tory, Jacqueline was not necessarily a model
guest and my mother, unavoidably guilty of
deserting the city, didn't know which side to
take when my friend claimed we should all
combine forces, abolish boundaries, embrace
the Yuoangui, and finally see and take note of
what the people who lived on our borders
looked like. A still more uncivilized guest was

brandishing a newspaper, some mines broken
free of their line had killed a whole group of
sea lions whose mangled bodies were most
unpleasantly enmeshed in the beachgoers'
palm trees, the sea lions were, in general, a
consensual subject that my mother tried in
vain to agree with once more while a city
councilman (who, incidentally, had known my
husband well) threatened to leave the table if
Jacqueline and the guest with the questionable
taste did not put a brake on their rude imagi-
nations. My mother, vexed by the lack of interest in herself, exclaimed all at once (thus do
the last shreds of our certainties melt away)
that her psychic (my mother plunged in the
depths of a crystal ball while a depraved
Yuoangui patted her shoulder) had predicted
to her, I couldn't hear the rest, the city councilman was getting up, in the sudden chaos I
thought that the table, occupied by knocking
spirits, was going to count out our dead and fly
away, shattering the windowpanes, but that
was not the course events took. I remained in
my chair, my thighs caressed by the brouhaha
that undulated beneath the tablecloth, my
bottom firmly settled, a little drunk; and it
wasn't the table, remarkably stable beneath
my elbows, that was turning, but all the rest
around me, the guests in their hullabaloo, the

shards of light projected onto the walls by my mother's liquid dress, the light fixtures swinging like a pendulum beneath Jacqueline's strident intonations, and the appalled countenance of my mother-in-law, who may simply have been waiting for the roast. And it seemed to me that all this agitation had broken out for a single purpose: to mask my husband's absence beneath the hue and cry, to fill with roiling air and gesticulating arms the insane gulf his vanished molecules had left behind.

I saw the broad, red faces, the violet mouths, the hands very close to me, the fingers through which I examined, as under an infrared microscope, the nerve impulses sprung from the brain; and the bodies jutting forward, legs planted below, torsos cut off by the table cloth, and the great movement that swept all of it along, setting in motion and maintaining the charge of atoms of every kind of matter: a mist of sweat, keratin and squamae glossier than the undersides of mushrooms that floated among the bodies, amid the spray of sputtered alcohol: the furniture, slowly falling apart in vegetal cinders beneath the jagged teeth of acarids; the wine, gathered and enclosed in glasses smeary with fingerprints; the carbon dioxide that was thickening the air, each of its molecules sys-

tematically taking the place of two oxygen
atoms at every exhalation, so that at this pace
we would soon be nothing but bluish shapes,
our pulses slowed, our hearts thickened, our
tongues coated with black. All these atoms
were mingling in the test tube of the main
room, an audacious chemistry was combining
new forms of matter: from a nanometer of
maternal eyelash and a mol of sofa (or fish or
silicone or councilman) was born a minuscule
hypothesis, a potential of something in suspension in the air or burrowed in the carpet,
its flagella wriggling virtually with hope; and
without making a move, prostrate on the sofa,
I witnessed the eruption of a crude will, engulfed there like a glacial wind, issued from
what window, what fireplace, what ocean,
which instantly drove out the germinating
micro-monster and prohibited it from being.
But none of the guests seemed the least bit
concerned by the carnage nor by the
nor'wester belched out by this poster dragon
whose breath flowed ceaselessly and irremedi-
ably between the atoms of our space.

It then became clear to me that my mother,
Jacqueline, the councilman, and the guests
(all prettily powdered with an agitation that
was nothing but a sneeze), weren't hiding anything beneath their dispute: what they were

debating indeed occupied them more or less,
and had nothing to do with either my husband
or, strictly speaking, the monsters or the
dragon. In the haze around them I saw the
outline of certain of their thoughts, a betwixt
and between of bodies, gestures, and words; a
whole fog bank of molecules that sometimes
condensed into brief white curlicues, or humid
flashes of lightning, or could float for brief
periods like a memory of my husband, and the
awkward consciousness of a lack or a malaise
(of the sort I had believed I felt at the very
beginning of the evening). Yet the arguments
went on, in their roundness the curlicues by-
passed the void's obstacle, and the bodies were
moving without too many jolts. And I thought
I understood, in that part of them that resisted
unraveling, that neither my mother nor Jacqueline nor any of the guests (except perhaps
my mother-in-law) had any exact memory of
my husband. Certainly they knew I had been
married, that my husband had disappeared,
and that undoubtedly I was suffering from
that fact; but to all appearances they were
incapable of putting themselves there; they
were barred from recovering the two of us in
our interrupted course. It was physics, the
physics of the moment, and also the physics
that describes the laws of memory, absence,

and disappearances. When he evaporated, my
husband had taken with him, as a comet car-
ries along its tail, all the atmosphere that made
him be himself; nothing of him remained
except me and I was deprived of the air I once
had breathed and that no one could infuse me
with in his place. Not that our love had been
this or that ("our love" is a tired expression),
nor, fundamentally, that we were unique: my
husband was not irreplaceable for me nor I
for him, and I'm sure, now, that we were like
everyone, if it's true that everyone, after a
second of silence, hesitates to say "our love."
But the space he left remained empty, a yawn-
ing hole in the universe, and that was the
scandal that no law known to me could describe, make up for, or punish.

*T*he city councilman walked out, his
wife babbled excuses, snatched the
coat that my mother, bedecked in spiraling
silicone, held out to her. There was a movement of slow fallout. And I saw, indeed, in the
guests' calm reassumption of their seats and in
the good humor with which they retrieved
their cutlery, accepted some wine, smiled at
everything that had just happened, the cloud
of something that was settling. The air around
us took on a strange purity like those pierc-

ingly vivid skies that the sun does not warm,
and beneath which you come to understand
that blue is the color of the void. When nothing was left in suspension, when the air was
entirely calm and clear between each chair
and each body, silence fell like a rock. Then
the door at the back of the room opened very
slowly (time began distending), I thought the
city councilman was coming back to offer his
apologies or kill all the guests, who were looking at each other in embarrassment, giving
little coughs and ahems, while my mother was
undoubtedly inspired to hold forth on the passage of angels; I thought then that I was the
only one to see my husband come in, but the
cry my mother-in-law let out immediately
disproved that hypothesis. While the guests
huddled around her swooning form, my husband seemed to hesitate, trembling on the
threshold. I distinctly felt the strong current of
air that preceded him, though no lampshade
moved, the tablecloth was unfluttered, and no
one, supposing that the general attention
could have turned for one second away from
my mother-in-law, called for the door to be
shut. My husband was looking at me with a
strange look, as in the photographs where he
seemed to be staring at a point behind the
lens. I tried to meet his glance, to intercept it

before the invisible surveyor's rod his eyes
were seeking slid too far away. I took a step
forward; my husband didn't move. Very
slowly I reached out my hand. We were about
ten meters apart: the width of the table, the
carpet, the corner of the entryway, a hat
stand. Slowly I initiated the maneuver. I did
not take my eyes off him, it seemed to me that
this was a way of keeping him there; like a
figure you've just barely discerned in a carpet,
emerging from the woolen interlacement of
lines and dots, a face that no one has know-
ingly woven there, and that you'll lose if you
blink. And my husband had, so to speak, the
consistency of such figures in carpets (in
stucco, in burls, in the fluctuations of clouds).
His outline was broken and scattered, his coat
fluffed and frothed around him, his hair
floated above his head like a pulverization
and the skin of his face was sprinkled with a
vaporous and very white hue. I glided slowly
around the table, forcing myself not to lose
sight of his features; my memory was helping
me as much as my eyes. He absolutely had to
stay there, one more second, until I touched
him, still another second, despite the uncer-
tainty of whatever it was in him that seemed
to deny to time the possibility of making him
last and to space the possibility of giving him

a form. A streetlight outside filtered through
him like the sun beneath the rising mist of a
very cold morning; his eyes, which did not
look at me, which looked through me, were
full of that same mist. My husband, despite
his luminous hue, looked anxious and
washed-out.

I had made my way around the table. I was
setting out across the carpet. My eyes were not
enough to seize him; I had to enfold him in my
arms, and he would rest, he would lean against
me, tired, his head heavy, and we would go
home. I would love him my whole life. I would
take care of him. I would worry about his
health, his work, his solitude, and the void
that he might experience. I would ask him to
describe the houses, the streets, the fountains,
and the sky to me, and his dreams of what our
children would be like. We would talk about
everything. We would not be afraid of weep-
ing. We would see the same colors, the same
shapes, and I would stop wondering if my
husband (if cats, birds, fish, and flies with
their many-faceted eyes) felt and saw what I
felt and saw. The carpet slowly paraded past
beneath my feet and my husband remained at
the threshold, immobile, within reach of my
hand yet still as far away, still withdrawn to
the same silent distance. The weft stretched

away before me. The designs grew larger,
more complicated, intertangled, I followed a
blue line that suddenly coiled around a green
one, and I didn't know if I was the victim of an
enchantment woven into the wool, of my own
impatience to be with him, or of something
between us that had loosened the threads of
time and space. I mouthed his name in silence,
terrified to speak it aloud; everything had to
be silent, everything had to remain at the same
level of bubbling hubbub, sounds of lapping
water and limbo; nothing must bang, not a
door, not a name, or my husband would fly
away like a bird that has already crossed
oceans.

There was only an arm's length left to the
hat stand, the width of a floorboard, a single
stride to the entryway, I was going to take him
in my arms and shut the door with a kick so
the draft would no longer threaten to disperse
him to the four winds. I thought I had reached
the fringes of the carpet. My husband moved
back. Something moved with him, an ebb
of air, he had moved like the images on old
computer monitors that leave a train behind
them in the pixels, the impression lingering
where the contact no longer is; a glow that
reassembles as soon as the motion has
stopped. But my husband was still trembling,

blurred and indefinite, as if subject to bugs in
the program of his existence. He would have
to be redesigned, enclosed, reduced, finally
made to stay there, compressed into the sharp
outlines of a body and newly unmolded so he
would stop fluttering in place like air flying
with dust above a shaken rag. I touched the
corner of the entryway, the hat stand rose up
in the combat posture of a crab, hooks, coat
pegs, and hoops reaching to poke out my eye,
I pushed it over, there was an enormous noise,
my mother-in-law cried out once more, and
huge bubbles burst into various voices in my
ears. I had the time to seize a light like a
shower of sequins that stayed on my fingers
and in my eyes: a powdery streak, a snowfall
of air, and I very distinctly felt the thickness of
something that followed my husband and took
him from me and emptied me of my substance
(doubled up in the pit of my stomach, it
stopped beating).

X

Somebody shut that door, a voice said. Through the gaps among the branches, I stared up at the blackness of the sky over the even blacker garden. A rustling reached me, the flutter of a wing already scattered, Jacqueline took my arm, *your mother-in-law*, she said. The mother of my husband, as diaphanous as her son, was stretched on the sofa, people were fanning her, offering her something to drink, my mother was hopping up and down, a telephone jammed at her ear, signaling me to do my share for this hysteric, since responsibility for her obviously fell to me. Jacqueline drove us both back to our respective neighborhoods. I don't know why I didn't go right home, I acted as if I were opening the door of my building under my friend's

watchful gaze, then, once her car had gone
around the corner, pulled my key out of the
lock and walked away. I must have walked for
a long time. I was back at the seashore. We
had only taken that long walk once, my husband and I, from our house to the sea. It was a
summer day and we had gone swimming, and
all the way back we felt the pull of the tide;
the dust among the dunes became asphalt,
the salt stretched out our cheeks, the red sun
covered us with a fine tracery of cracks. I
remember the shower when we got back, the
feeling of drinking through my pores. I don't
remember if we made love. I remember events
but love was not an event, it was more like a
particular form of time, that we left and came
back to or that left us and came back to us: a
time that appeared to be unified but that may
have followed certain inflections and curves
like the movement of a year, a revolution
around something, we approached and then
slowly moved away from a point that, by
seasons, starts, or twists, was warmer, more
sensitive, more central. I don't remember particular nights (except for places, hotel rooms,
only rarely beaches: superimposed episodes); I
remember periods, passages, smells, damp-
nesses, tensions or avoidances, nuances and
approaches, drowsinesses and awakenings;

always more or less the same, but the more or less is what gives a rhythm to this memory. Facing the nocturnal sea, I understood that it was lost time. The memory of my lovers was identifiable, I could revive it, take it out and handle it, still take pleasure from it, rub my remembering mind up against it. The time of my husband was diffuse, a single line of time that I couldn't retrieve in the unwinding of memory, but that seemed woven into its very fiber, impossible to undo and recognize.

The dark mass of the sea beat at my temples. The only thing that turned inside me was a generalized movement that all at once, like an implosion occupying a vacuum, became a nostalgia that was horrible because it had no object. It was fear and not desire, fear of having lost the point of the desire. The desire was so vast, my wait become universal, that I felt in my body and in all that I was a kind of detachment, a flight that was empty and aimless, just as, in a nightmare, we believe we are approaching a point that always recedes back to half the distance away and leaves you there, driven mad, incapable of understanding that you will not reach it. Was it possible that my husband would never come back? Days had gone by, but the idea was still new: a sorrow endlessly recommencing, intact,

that took up all of space: always just as perfectly in the same way, in lieu and in place of
memory, I suffered.

I sat down on a ridge of the dune and lit
a cigarette. It was a gesture I had gone
back to, a habit of my own. The apartment
was haunted by double gestures, split in two
by my husband's absence; smoking instituted
a different era, but one in which it was equally
impossible to live. Time no longer passed. A
cigarette, another, my breathing seemed
always to pick up at the same point. I saw only
the sea, sinking slowly beneath the sky, which
may have begun to grow lighter. A fire had
been lit in the distance, in a brazier beside the
blockhouses. The wind brought me bursts of
voices. To sleep outside from now on, to be
murdered, or to run into the waves and drown
all became a possibility, a single and indifferent way out, the idea that here, perhaps, was a
plan, something to decide on and set in place
myself. The sea lions were snoring in a heap
like so many fat hens. The moon had fallen to
the other side of the earth, and the surf could
be glimpsed only by the gleam of the last
stars, its rumble gave notice, in snatches, of
the bursts of white foam. The sea was more
enormous than ever in the night, limitless be-

neath the sky it swallowed up; you had to
think a little before deciding where the stars
were, agreeing to place a limit on the sea's
height. It was comforting that the sea was so
large, so incomprehensibly large. Not understanding the sea—that was something you
could accept. You could tell yourself stories
and let yourself be rocked, tell yourself that
the sea was a memory, that every molecule of
seawater in the sea was a parcel of memory,
lost but found again there, reassembled between shores, navigable and as vast as you
could hope.

T took a taxi home. Daylight was breaking through, opposite the sea's west. The
building stood out very sharply, a black block
rimmed with light, its facade invisible in the
shadow. Only the glow of a night-light could
be made out at the windows of our apartment,
because I hadn't closed the shutters, and that
made a kind of eye, a single eye, open and
watchful. I sat down on the sidewalk across
the way. The street was narrow and the wall
leaned over me. Our foreshortened windows
glimmered, a dark blue line above an edge.
The halo that was filtering out from behind
the building made it even darker, I felt as if it
were going to pluck me between two fingers,

knee resting on the ground, and pull me up to
its eye. The indifferent sun continued to
climb. The window of the sixth floor opened,
casting a faint light across the facade like
makeup floating around an eyelid. Someone
was smoking a cigarette, elbows on the windowsill, gray clouds of breath melting into the
blackness of the upper floors. I had risen to
my feet. A second silhouette seemed to take
shape beside the first, very close. That was
undoubtedly the sound of a conversation I was
now hearing, in scratches against the facade. I
went up. My legs hardly obeyed me. The stairway unwound beneath my feet, but the land-
ings didn't succeed one another. I felt as if I
had been climbing for a long time already, and
yet I had become mired in an unrecognizable
mezzanine, or else I was going down to the
cellar where something still more bewildering,
I couldn't imagine what, awaited me. I
stopped for a second, breathless. The empty
space at the heart of the stairway, caught in
the ribbon of the banister, lost its verticality.
The walls took on new curves, as if the steps,
in addition to winding in on themselves, were
coiling in the hollow of a spiraling axis; the
stairwell, too, had the shape of a snail, though
I was unable to confirm that: the stairway I
was climbing seemed to carry on regularly,

but the larger stairway it was part of must
have risen or descended in loops, without it
being possible for me to know where I was;
this second stairway was perhaps also subject
to the twisting of a third large stairway, and so
on, to what floor or depth and in what direction I don't know. In my deserted apartment, I
tried many times to sketch this sensation,
which escapes my understanding, the most
successful attempt being more or less this:

The electric light multiplied by the tortoiseshell light fixture hurt my eyes. How
much time would you need to go anywhere if
you had to climb the stairway rooted at the
center of the whole encagement? I began
pacing through the apartment. The carpet was
strewn with balled-up papers, I gave little
kicks that stirred up ephemeral snow flurries.
I hadn't unearthed anyone in our two rooms,
not in the kitchen, not in the closets; no one

who might have been there, not a pair of
ghosts, a monster, a joke, a hoax, nothing.

I spent a while stretched out on the bed.
The lightbulbs hung straight down. I felt the
walls sloping again; the bed rose toward the
ceiling, the ceiling fell toward the yucca,
which creaked as it grew; the space between
the bed and the window shrank to the point
that the street seemed to originate beneath my
sheets, and the grid of the city to spring from
me like a net. The bed came so close to the
window that I thought it was going to break
open the glass and carry me off, sheets floating in the wind, me clutching the pillow. The
boulevards stretched out into the black sky,
garlands of streetlights fell from my lighted
windows, the monuments stood out, sculp-
tures in the round against the horizon. I felt
the pressure of air under my pillow, pitching
under the bed, and if I stretched out my arms I
could lean against the speed of currents of air,
I could take advantage of the ascending movement, by slight quiverings I would know how
to tell the hot air that rises from the cold air
that descends, and in the hollow of my palms,
under my arms, under my belly, holding up
my heels, flowing between my fingers, I could
experience the slipstream of my flight. At the
end, limpid, was the sea. By looking only at

the sky I could imagine it, the sea, beating at
the foot of the building, I heard the breathing
of surf in the lobby, the door smashed in and
shells encrusting the stone little by little (taxis
weighed anchor, their passengers, wearing
raingear, stepped through windows, bakers
brought up from cellars flour heavy with gorg-
ing shrimp). There needed to be a flood, a
sudden erosion of the dunes, a melting of the
glaciers, I thought I would finally overflow,
something in me would give way, and there
would be nothing left for me to do but float
with the sea lions. A light wind made my windowpanes tinkle. I became aware that the sun
hadn't risen: either my sketching had taken
me so much time that night had fallen and I
hadn't followed the rotation of the planet or,
on the contrary, only a few minutes had gone
by since I came up. The surf had calmed
down, something in the lightbulbs was gently
going out. I turned toward the window and
saw my husband, perched on the guardrail. I
got up to let him in, he stepped over the edge
and took off his coat, which I took from his
hands. I told him I had been waiting for him a
long time. He didn't answer. Sitting on the
edge of the bed, shoes on the carpet, he
seemed to be waiting for something, as if it
were up to me to welcome him, to ask him,

what do I know, if he had had a nice trip. I
stood there, smoothing out his coat, looking
for a word, a remark. Finally I draped his coat
over the headboard of the bed and sat down.
We sat there in silence. From time to time I
risked a sidelong glance at him, not knowing
if it was up to him or up to me to reach out the
arms, caress, murmur apologies, reproaches,
vows, those words we never spoke; to lie down
while I undid a first button, pulling on a first
sleeve; or perhaps to bang on the walls, stamp,
hurl objects across the room. The fact was, as I
covertly observed my husband, my husband
whom I had known for seven years, with
whom I had brushed my teeth, bemoaned my
fate, scratched backs, intertwined tongues,
and squabbled over baguettes, that I no longer
knew what to do or who I was dealing with. To
my first impression of blurriness was now
added a certain heaviness, an out-of-the-
ordinary heaviness that far from stabilizing
his image diffracted it even more: immobile or
wrapped up in his coat as before, my husband
still made an acceptable spouse; but if he
stirred even an eyelid, whatever it was that
kept him there all the same seemed to weigh
down at the center of his person, to increase
the density of its matter, to gather him into a
single central point which left him practically

empty along the edges (a long-haired animal
with a strong light shining from behind whose
halo of fur, now forming only an outline,
reveals a ridiculously skinny body; a
marble—of the kind known, on playgrounds,
as cat's eyes—shot through with glints of
light, left lying in the sun on a mirrored surface, and whose colorful shadow shifts the
nuances to create a very broad virtual marble
with an opaque, minuscule heart that is the
sum of all its colors; a scene in a movie shown
in slow motion and shot at too slow a time, the
exposed film overflows onto the movement
and looks as if it precedes it, foresees what will
follow, how the shot body will pour out onto
the ground, tracing the inflections of its fall in
space, a gradation of a falling body; or, if you
like, a wave that rises up and is pierced by a
ray of light, the water takes on a green so bril-
liant that it is no longer anything but a white
light, neither wave nor sun can be seen, only
an absence displaced around a rotating center,
and from wave to wave you lose the sea). My
husband, sitting there so nicely on the bed,
wearing the pants I knew so well, his polished
shoes treading the carpet, his loosened tie and
day's growth of beard exactly as they were
when he went down to get the baguette, my
husband made my eyes ache and spilled out

around himself so much that I imagined myself easily passing my hand through his body
and tickling him in the back. To take him in
my arms had at first struck me as a simple and
soothing solution, his outline remained more
or less definite, even if its contents seemed
alternately to overflow it or to shrink; but I
was afraid of grasping him only to discover
that he was not there, finding myself closing
my grip on a precipitate of him, a fossilized
extract that supposedly epitomized him, the
DNA of a ghost, a mindless twist of matter I
wouldn't have known what to do with except
put it on a shelf to gather dust. I wondered
what my husband looked like naked. His
clothes (his shirt, his tie half undone, his
pants, his socks and shoes) put a filter between
me and his substance, and while they, too,
appeared to be subject to the general rule of
halftones (the shirt gone pale, the hesitant tie,
the hovering pants, the shoes lost in their own
shine), they seemed better able to resist disappearance. What was the texture of my husband's body? How thick was his skin now?
How did it smell? And if I went to him, if I
succeeded in burying myself against him, how
would he react? Did I still need only to climb
in his lap, wrap my arms around him, and
crush my breasts against him in order to feel

him, upright and surging? I wanted to kiss
that skin; I wanted to caress what his clothing
barely concealed. I wanted nothing to do with
a husband I couldn't hold in my arms.

He stood up slowly. Yet, slow as the movement was, I registered only a kind of unfolding
of space, as if his body, in addition to standing
up, had displaced the dimensions in order to
find its problematic place within them. Space
seemed to regroup around him, making
another hasty sketch of him, allowing for his
height, width, and depth; yet the walls looked
perplexed as to the position they should take.
What remained behind, like the streak of a
meteorite, floated at his back, forming a kind
of brilliance that radiated heat into the
heavier air around it, and that could just as
easily have looked like wings, a jet pack, a
propeller, a parachute, a dragonfly's buzzing
wings, a lawn-mower motor, or anything else
that can be carried on the back and may have
an aptitude for flight. And when I felt my husband encircle me simply by extending his
barely material hands, and charge me in turn
with that particular energy (he was so close
that he was almost invisible, and strictly
speaking he didn't touch me, but I felt him: at
once entirely within me and somewhere where
I could not reach him), when I merged with

his nebula, I missed the time when I could curl up in his arms unproblematically, but I also knew myself to be overwhelmed by the impatient pull of two hundred kites.

I never understood if we passed right through the window or if my husband opened it to let us out. All I know is that when I found myself back on my bed, alone, spangled with something that truly happened (I remember especially and with some embarrassment my voice begging him to teach me to fly), still charged with an energy that pounded at me whenever I touched the bed (the wall, the door, the headboard where his coat still lay), when I found myself alone again in the stammering light of dawn, and with sober powerlessness pictured myself making coffee, seeing my mother off on her boat, and going back to the agency to write this story, at that moment I stopped wondering whether my husband (or cats, birds, fish, and flies with their many-faceted eyes) felt and saw what I felt and saw.